Many Long Years to Home

Many Long Years to Home

A Novel

Mary M. Flad

Epigraph Books
Rhinebeck, New York

Paperback ISBN 978-1-960090-92-8

Book design by Colin Rolfe

Epigraph Books
22 East Market Street, Suite 304
Rhinebeck, New York 12572
(845) 876-4861
epigraphpublishing.com

Dedicated to the memory of all of the immigrant women who have become the foundation of the modern nursing profession.

Contents

DUBLIN, IRELAND,
1833–1844

NEW HAVEN, CONNECTICUT,
1844–1868

FERMOY, COUNTY CORK, IRELAND

1813

A Door Closes,
Another Opens

Margaret ran her fingers through her hair, long and straight, tangled after a night of restless sleep. This small space, a small stone house on a street in Fermoy, in County Cork in the south of Ireland, had been her world since she had been born. Everything was secure and predictable, and now she was fourteen, old enough to be impatient with the sameness of it all. Michael her brother seemed quite satisfied that he knew what the future held for him: Uncle John's farm, with its potatoes and a cow or two, and a daily regularity of what was to be done, the sun rising and setting and the seasons moving from one to another. She was different: she wanted a life with some uncertainties, something changeable. Something in her wanted to learn new skills, to become competent, useful, valued.

Things were happening that she did not understand. The conversation between her mother, Kathleen, and Captain Alexander Augustine Hickey her father had changed, as if they were strangers rather than husband and wife. Alexander's eyes had looked blank, withdrawn, rather than engaging Margaret's when she read psalms to him last evening from the prayer book. Her mother was the same as she had always been, but new worries creased her brow.

What would it be like, Margaret wondered, to have dozens of books, lined up on a shelf or piled beside her bed, every one of them filled with stories of fantastic places or great adventures. When she traced out the words in her father's prayer book, she loved the look and the sound of them. But she wanted to read something more than prayers and psalms. She had heard stories of people traveling to distant lands – people from

Cork city, even people from Fermoy and the other towns along the Blackwater. Someday, she resolved, that will be me. I will go to Dublin, to London, to Paris, even to America. I will not spend my life on a farm tending the chickens.

"Da," she said to Alexander when she finished reading, "Tell me about America."

He looked toward his daughter with confusion. His time in America was years in the past. She was not Abigail, but there was something about her that rekindled the memory of another place, another time. The line was blurred between <u>now</u> and <u>then</u>. He could see the long lines of men in red coats, and the German troops behind them marching to the music of their own band, and the following throng of women and children, with wagons of cooking-pots and laundry tubs, foodstuffs and tent-posts and bedding. Thousands and thousands, some marching, some straggling, along the path from Canada to the expected victory in New York. He had been posted at Ticonderoga, and then his orders were to move with the advance, to oversee the construction of defenses wherever the battlefield might be. He had never spoken of it, of building battlements and of the weeks of fighting and then the long cold march to Boston, the months of freezing in a makeshift camp, the illness, the coughing, the fever, the death. It was nothing to be remembered, but now it was fresh in his mind, the only thing he could remember with any certainty.

"America. I was a young man then, in His Majesty's army, and I spent five years, maybe more. . . . it is a vast place, and no longer is it our land. Many people died; I watched them die on either side of me." He had never said these things aloud before; they had been pushed out of his mind for all these years. "Abigail," he said, "She was a young girl, a little older than you, with a laugh like music, and she worked at the cooking-fires and made it seem that there could be joy and loveliness in the midst of all that misery and bloodshed. And then, after we were defeated in the great battle at Saratoga, when I found that she was still alive, and I was alive too, just barely so, we promised to care for each other through all the miseries that might befall us. And so we did, through that wretched winter, and then in February she sickened, and before the spring came, she died. And that is all I know of America." He stopped speaking, and turned toward the window.

Kathleen heard the words, although they were not spoken to her. Or to anyone, except himself. Margaret heard them, as if they were words written on a page, explaining a small piece of a distant history.

Alexander also heard them, not sure if they were said with his own voice, but certain they were true, even if something he had almost forgotten. The voice went on, but now only in his mind, inaudible to the others:

> 'Tis a chill wind at Crown Point, whether winter or summer, and whether it blows from the north or the west. When we first marched south along the lake, a long arduous journey from Canada, the sight of the high embankments of the fort was a blessing, for it looked as if they would provide shelter from the wind. But that was not true: inside the fortifications the wind howled as much as it had outside, and even within the sturdy stone barracks it seemed that the gales could penetrate.

> If I wandered into the hills, with a party of men to gather wood for fuel, or by myself with a fishing rod, it was possible to escape from the wind, at least for a short while. But the fort in its exposed location, with a clear line of sight across the waters to the north, had no protection; nor did any of us residing there.

> Who can say what might have happened if we had remained there longer, holding firm to it against both the winds and the rebels? More men thrown into madness by the constant blowing, of course; but the humiliation of capture by Ethan Allen and his band of drunken zealots would have been less definitive, less final. Once Ticonderoga fell to them we had no recourse, no path of retreat.

> I was saved at Ticonderoga only because of my fishing rod, which had me wandering off on a fine spring day in search of a brook to throw a line into. The snow was

sufficiently melted that I could make my way, and I caught a respectable line of trout – close to a dozen of them – before I returned toward the fort across the flatlands to its south. As I drew near I could hear that something was amiss: pandemonium, shouting by uncouth and unfamiliar voices. I thought it best to take my trout elsewhere, until I could learn the nature and cause of the upheaval.

The first farm I came to, heading toward the town, had a hay barn that could provide me shelter and a hiding place; but even better to get my fish cooked as well. And so I knocked on the door of the house, and asked the madam if they would let me stay in their barn a night or two in return for a fine meal of trout. Who could resist the offer? And so she cooked the trout, and I stayed in the hayloft, and in the course of all this met Abigail the daughter.

She was not someone who would have run off because of her own impulses, however bleak and lonely farm life near the foot of Lake Champlain might be. But she saw me as a handsome adventurer, not a cowardly soldier, which might have been closer to the truth. And so when I found that my compatriots at Ticonderoga had been marched off in ignominy, leaving the fortress to Allen's ragged bunch, I resolved to set off to locate some other British troops to which I could attach myself; and she impetuously left her parents and her home to follow me, certain that she would find a way to make herself useful. Which she did, for the almost three years until the fever took her, leaving me with the pain of her memory.

He heard the voice no more, and he had returned to his silence, his sitting and looking out the window, watching the rain and the partly-finished stone walls beyond the rain. Margaret closed the prayer book, and laid it down on the box beside his chair. Everything was the same as always, but everything had changed.

Kathleen tested the potatoes, boiling in the pot atop the stove. She knew that Alexander had a past, though she knew little about it. As did she herself: in Ireland, a woman who married a British soldier had a past, not a future. Michael's father, Brendan the fisherman, had been her first and only love. He had become a fisherman because that was the thing that men did who lived near the coves and rocky shoreline along Ireland's southwest coast, and they went out into the tumultuous waters and came home with their boats full of fish. Almost always they came home.

Perhaps his name was a portent of what sometimes happened – the times when, like Saint Brendan, the small rough curraghs would set forth on a sunny morning and as the day progressed the wind would howl and the sky darken to a purple almost black and the boats race for home, most of them, but not all of them, and it was never known if instead they had reached another shore, or were simply gone into the deep.

To put the water on the stove, a pot of scrubbed potatoes, and watch them come to a boil and then wait, endlessly, endlessly, for them to be sufficiently cooked to be eaten – that was something she had done over and over again since she was a young girl. Kathleen went through it without even thinking: counting the people who would be at the table, counting the potatoes, scrubbing them, bringing them to a boil, poking them with a fork to determine that they were sufficiently cooked to be enjoyed. Sometimes potatoes were the whole meal, perhaps with a bit of butter; sometimes there was also a fish, or cabbage, or chicken, or egg. But always, quite predictably, there would be potatoes.

DONALDSTOWN,
COUNTY TIPPERARY,
IRELAND
1813–1820

Housecleaning

Margaret smoothed her skirt in her lap, and adjusted the shawl around her shoulders as it slipped down from her head. This was not her accustomed dress: part of her still felt to be a child, ready to skip and hop along a pathway. Sitting in the carriage beside her mother, she clutched the handle of the carpetbag, which rested on the floor at her feet.

The horse pulling the open cart was chestnut brown, with black markings along its mane. The driver seemed pleased to be carrying more than just packages on the ride back to Donaldstown from town: bringing two ladies, one of them quite young, was an unusual occasion. "William is my name, mum," he said to Kathleen as he helped her up the precarious back step of the jaunting cart, and pushed the packages aside so that she and Margaret could seat themselves on the side benches. "Not that the ride is comfortable, what with the condition of the road and all, but it won't be long." He climbed into his seat, picking up the reins. "Sir Harry here, he's a good horse, but not the fastest mode of transportation. But he will get us there safe and sound." Kathleen and Margaret clutched the backs of their seats, as the cart bumped its way along the road northward.

Dr. George Powers and his wife Elizabeth, and the doctor's elderly mother Lady Amelia, were the people who lived in the great house behind the long gray stone wall on the north road to Donaldstown, a place that had become their home only recently. It was built because of the grandiose and irrational dreams of another Englishman, Hubert Winston, who thought that money simply was there to be found like the stones in the field. The day came, after the enormous house was built and the miles of walls around it, when Lord Hubert Winston ran out of money, and ran out of horses to race or to ride to hounds, and ran out of luck, and ran out of the days of his life, and died. Sell it, his sister Lady Amelia was advised, but who would buy such a grandiose monstrosity at the ends of the earth, beyond reach of civilized society? More likely it would just be left to fall down.

For thirty-five years, Dr. Powers and his wife Elizabeth had lived quietly in their home in Dublin, behind the painted door and Palladian window of a Georgian-style brick house on a street convenient to the Dublin hospital, and within a reasonable distance of the Kilmainham hospital as well. Their life had been quieter than they had hoped: no children came to them, but they continued to enjoy each other's company. Lady Amelia had come from London to join them only reluctantly, several years after the death of her husband. Moving to Ireland was, she reasoned with herself, a certain kind of death, a start on the journey to rejoin her beloved Duncan, who had always treated her with such love and consideration, indulging her obsession with fine porcelain and crystal. Sir Duncan had been in an advantageous position to satisfy her love of porcelain, in particular: his interests in the East India Company had made it easy to acquire vases, bowls and even lidded boxes of unusual quality from the thriving trade with Asia. Crystal was available closer at hand, and he had seen to it that candlesticks, goblets, and a perfectly beautiful chandelier had arrived at their home in observance of special occasions such as anniversaries.

When Lady Amelia came somewhat unwillingly to Dublin, to take up residence with her son and daughter-in-law, all of this was left behind in storage – never, she was sure, would she see her treasures again in this lifetime. She did not want to think about whether they could or would accompany her to the hereafter; but she knew that in the stark simplicity of George and Elizabeth's dwelling they would have no place at all.

The whole question of the house – a mansion, really, almost a castle – at Donaldstown was fraught with dilemmas and possibilities for each of the three of them. Dr. George Powers was quite willing to move to a less exhausting routine than the slums and hospitals of Dublin had provided for him. Anyplace, he knew, would always have sick people needing care; and a military barracks not far away would assure that there would be a steady stream of injuries, whether from backfiring blunderbusses or drunken brawls, that would require treatment for which some compensation could be assured. Lady Amelia thought of the move to her late brother's house as one more interval on her journey to the Great Beyond, but it would also make it possible for her to send for her treasures of porcelain and crystal and display them properly, even though few visitors would come to gaze on them. And Elizabeth would miss the familiar streets of Dublin, but not its dirt and noise. Her time would be well spent in redeeming the walled garden that had gone to rack and ruin, pruning the roses and coaxing them back to life and beauty.

When Kathleen had heard that Dr. George Powers, recently arrived to the estate in Donaldstown, would be paying weekly visits to the garrison in Fermoy to see those among the troops and their dependents who might need care, she had persuaded Alexander to seek an appointment to see him, and accompanied him herself. At one moment he was quite lucid, the person she had known and lived with for the last decade and a half, and at other times he seemed to slip away, to barely recognize her or his surroundings.

Dr. Powers had made a simple proposition when Kathleen had appeared with Alexander for the second appointment. Given the uncertainties of their life, he wished to offer her and her daughter a few days of work, assisting his wife with the task of cleaning the entry hall of his new home, which had fallen into neglect in recent years. Alexander could remain at home, in his familiar setting: with their son Michael at hand everything would be close to its usual routine.

"'Tis a grand house, mum, if somewhat fallen to rack and ruin in recent years," William said, turning in his seat toward Kathleen as they passed through the great front gate and started along the entry lane lined with oaks and linden trees. Meadows stretched east and west beyond the line of trees; and at the end of the long drive was an enormous and forbidding edifice, grand beyond any building which either Kathleen or Margaret had entered before.

Once they passed the great stone wall and the iron gates, it was as if they were in a new and unfamiliar world. The gravel drive leading to the house was wide and straight and even, and made a great loop before the stairway leading to the massive front door. Another gravel drive, narrower and less impressive, led off from the loop around the east side of the house, and then on almost out of sight to the carriage barns and the servants' quarters. William circled the loop, quite aware that the building would make an awesome impression on his two passengers. He then followed the narrower drive, depositing them at the door of the kitchen wing – a door at ground level, with no elegant stairway leading to it.

The door led into a hallway, and off to the side was a large room warm with steam and smells delicious and unfamiliar. A large energetic woman with a ruddy face greeted them. "I am Jane Ellen, and you would be the two who milady Elizabeth expected would be arriving. You may leave your things here in the hallway: they will be perfectly safe. I will take you to meet her." She looked at them with an appraising eye, and said in a lower voice, "Milady does not expect people to curtsey to her, but this being the first time you're making her acquaintance, you might want to do so." Margaret looked questioningly at her mother: she knew nothing of curtseying, but was willing to learn.

"Thank you, mum," Kathleen responded, trying not to look as awkward as she felt. "We are pleased to be here, and hope we can be of use. It is a grand house, much larger than I could imagine."

"Too large to be of use to normal humankind," Jane Ellen said. "It is more than they could ever want, Dr. Powers and his family, but once a house is built, there it is, there's nothing to do but try to keep it from falling down around you. Whether they will succeed or not is another matter."

She led them along a dark corridor, up a narrow staircase, and through a door that opened into a wider hallway lined with windows, with a parlor off it that looked out into the walled garden. Elizabeth Powers sat by the window, reading in the sunshine as it broke through the clouds.

"Milady, Mrs. Hickey and her daughter have arrived," Jane Ellen said as they entered the room. Kathleen caught the sides of her skirt and curtseyed, and Margaret did her best to imitate without losing her balance. Elizabeth smiled and extended her hand.

"You see the challenge before me, Mrs. Hickey, and it is not one of my own choosing," Elizabeth said, greeting the two newcomers. "May I call you Kathleen? I am not comfortable with titles, however much they may be the custom. We are recently arrived in this place, as you know, and it will be years before it is fit to live in. Let me show you where the work must start." She walked out of the parlor, with Kathleen and Margaret following her, and proceeded to the heavy dark double doors at the end of the hall, and opened them before her. The room beyond was vast, and seemed even darker than the hue of the wooden doors. The smell of dust and damp greeted them, the odor of a place long closed up and unused.

Margaret and Kathleen stared into the dim cavern, with shadows of stag antlers and statuary casting ghostly presences against the high walls. After a moment or two of silence, Kathleen said briskly, "More light is needed in here. I will start with the windows. Is there a ladder that I can use?"

Elizabeth felt a wave of relief. "Yes, of course. A ladder, and a pail of water, and clean rags. That will be a start."

Kathleen realized that it would be her role to lay out the tasks, even though the list might be endless. "Margaret, the staircase is a good place for you to begin. First, clean the rail and the balustrades with a damp cloth, and then they will need to be rubbed with beeswax. The stairs themselves can be cleaned after the railing is finished."

It was a grand staircase, and the intricate carved railing was coated with dust and grime. It would be a full day's work, but there would be something to show for it at the end. Once the windows and the stairs had been dealt with, she would have a better sense of the enormity of the cleaning project, and how much the two of them could accomplish in a short time. "Start at the top, Margaret, so that the dirt moves downward and does not land on what you have already cleaned. It will take some rubbing: what is there has built up over the years, and it will take some encouragement to let loose its hold on the woodwork."

As the two of them set to work, Elizabeth first stood watching them and then, realizing that her watchfulness was contributing nothing to what was being accomplished, went back to her reading.

Lady Amelia soon interrupted her concentration. "Who are those women in the great hall? I have never seen them before. What is the reason we suddenly have strangers among us?"

Elizabeth had not thought that this might be an unwelcome disruption for anyone – in her own mind she had been pretending that the vast dark space was not even there, and now it was once again slowly emerging, like a new addition to their abode. That two cleaning-women would be disturbing, invaders in Lady Amelia's tranquil life, was a surprise.

"I am sorry I did not tell you beforehand. George has arranged for two people from Fermoy, Mrs. Hickey and her daughter, to begin the work of cleaning that huge room so that someday it will be fit to use once again. I am sorry that I did not realize their presence might bother you." Elizabeth laid down her book, and took Lady Amelia's hand. "Come now, so I can introduce them to you."

Perplexed, Lady Amelia walked with Elizabeth somewhat unwillingly. Why should she have to meet someone scrubbing the stairs, or washing the windowpanes? These things had to be done, but what did it matter who was doing them? They might not even speak the same language, and if they did, it was doubtful that they would have anything to say to each other. But she recognized that Elizabeth was trying to please her, to find a way that this house might be splendid once again, a place where porcelain and crystal might be laid out and admired, where the finer things in life, not just the garden with its cabbages and rosebushes, would receive the attention they deserved.

Margaret was sitting on the landing, rubbing vigorously at the indentations in the carved wood of the post where the stair changed direction, moving back into an angle of descent for the lower half of the staircase. Through the openings she could see her mother on the ladder at the window. The sun cast a patchwork of light and shadow on the floor – the leaded outline of the windowpanes, the steps and uprights of the ladder. It reminded her of the stepping-stones in her Uncle John's farmyard, an invitation to play, to hop and skip as a child. But today was not a day for child's play, and she luxuriated in this new thing, doing real work, almost like a grown-up. As the door opened and Elizabeth Powers entered, holding the hand of Lady Amelia, she looked down upon them, creatures from an unfamiliar world.

"Mrs. Hickey – Kathleen – this is Lady Amelia, by whose grace we have come to live in this lovely place," said Elizabeth. Kathleen came quickly down the ladder steps, wiping her wet hands against her skirt, then pushing her hair back from her face. "And where is your daughter? Ah, there you are, Margaret."

Kathleen curtseyed to Lady Amelia and said, "We are pleased to be here, mum." Elizabeth was smiling; Lady Amelia's lips were pursed, her only thought being that she wished to withdraw from this encounter, that she saw no necessity for any further conversation.

Margaret had come down the stairs and attempted a curtsey, careful of her balance, so that she would appear more graceful than she had earlier. Lady Amelia would prefer that she were not there at all; but she looked hard at the girl, wondering if she would have to see her again, or if she would mercifully disappear. The girl was thin, almost wiry, all angles. The child gave of more of an impression of energy than beauty. But her expression was pleasant and cheerful, nothing from which one could take offense, with no sign of impudence or ill manners. Just unpracticed in the finer things, unschooled, but not without promise. Lady Amelia inclined her head, a slight nod, to acknowledge that she had seen the two of them; but she could not bring herself to soften the pursed lips, to give even the hint of a smile.

Things change only slowly, thought Elizabeth. "You must be hungry," she said briskly. "Go down to the kitchen and Jane Ellen will have something to nourish you. And I will come again during the afternoon to see what progress you have made." She smiled, and took Lady Amelia's hand, and they turned and walked again through the large dark doors.

The mother and daughter looked uncertainly at each other, seeing themselves as different people than they had been while riding in the cart behind William early that morning. Margaret the child had always deferred in obedience to her mother; now there were other voices telling her what to do, and directing her mother as well. She was becoming a person apart. Kathleen was diminishing, and a new distance was growing between them.

Back they went through the great dark doors, then to the small doorway leading to the narrow stairs going downward, then down the steps toward the kitchen. As soon as Kathleen and Margaret were on the stairs, they could smell the kitchen and feel its steamy warmth. They stepped into the room, with its pots and pans hanging down along the walls, and the soft murmur of the stove and the whisper of steam from the tea kettle. The kitchen seemed to be empty, but then Margaret saw someone, a girl like herself, already sitting at the long plank table, which was set with bowls and spoons. They stood at the door, and then Jane Ellen came bustling down the hallway behind them, carrying an empty tray.

"Ready for something to eat, I see. You've had a busy morning. This here's Annie, my niece. Annie, say hello to Margaret: she's here for a bit to help with cleaning the great hall. Annie helps me wash up in the kitchen, and she takes care of the chickens as well."

Annie obediently slid out of her chair, eyeing Margaret with curiosity. "How old are you? I'm thirteen, going on fourteen. I came here last winter, after my mum got sick and died. Everyone here's old, you know that, don't you?" Her golden brown tousled curls framed a freckled face.

Jane Ellen ladled stew into the bowls – mutton, turnips, carrots, potatoes, hot and steaming, begging to be eaten. "There is soap next to the basin over near the window. Wash your hands and sit down; the stew needs a minute or two to cool. Will you both have tea?" She poured from the teapot into mugs at her own and Annie's places, and then the ones at the dishes set for Kathleen and Margaret, and then as William appeared, one more for him as well.

"Will you be my friend?" Annie said conspiratorially to Margaret who was now sitting next to her. "I haven't had a friend since I came here. I'll show you all my secret places."

Margaret looked at her silent and wide-eyed. She had never had a friend before – except, of course, her brother Michael. Her mother and father were different, not exactly friends. On the streets of Fermoy, and even on rare visits to her cousins, she was always the Redcoat's child, never someone chosen to play a game or sing a song with. She smiled. "I don't have a friend. I would like that very much." She picked up her spoon, hesitated, and then carefully chose a carrot swimming in her bowl of stew and lifted it to her mouth. It was delicious.

Jane Ellen had disappeared with an empty tray, and reappeared with it piled high with dirty dishes from the dining room. "Annie, be a good girl and wash out the pots, and then get these dishes washed and dried and put away. There's much to be done yet today."

The afternoon went quickly: the clean west windows, and the light of the afternoon sun, made the great hall less forbidding, less vast. The carved wood gleamed with the reflected glow from the windows. By the end of the day, Margaret had finished cleaning the rail on the left side of the stair, and was beginning to feel a certain pride in what she was doing. She liked things that were shining and beautiful, and without the dust all that was becoming evident.

The supper table held leftovers of the stew, this time with more potatoes, and a loaf of bread as well. After they ate Annie said, "Would you like to see my chickens? We have time before dark."

Margaret followed her out the door, the same door that she and her mother had entered early that morning. A breeze was already drying the puddles left by a rain shower. The fresh moist smell of the fields drifted in the air. Annie skipped along the path that led away from the house toward the barns and the kitchen garden, careful to avoid the droppings left by Sir Henry on the way to the carriage barn. Margaret began by walking properly and sedately, but in minutes was skipping as well, trying to keep up with her new friend, listening to a torrent of words as refreshing as the breeze itself.

Jane Ellen was not a person who ever sat down: as daylight faded at the kitchen window, she lit two more candles on the table, and continued wiping the counter surfaces beside the sink, and putting away the bowls and platters from the day's meals. "'Twould be fine for Margaret to be here with us for a time. She's a good girl, I can see; and this has been a lonely place for Annie, young as she is. It's no disgrace to be in service, and heaven knows there's work to be done here. When Lord Hubert was still alive it took twenty people to staff the household, what with guests coming and going, and race horses and great hunts, and banquets for half a hundred. We'll never see those days again, thank heaven. This is a much quieter time, with Dr. Powers busy with his work and devoted to his books as he is. And Lady Elizabeth is kind and not at all demanding."

Kathleen sat listening, her hands in her lap, her mind in turmoil.

These three or four days, work to be done kept her from the worry about what lay ahead; but suddenly, very soon, her child might no longer be with her.

"William has carried your bags upstairs, to a room next to the one where Annie stays. She can show you the way. I stay down here, in the room toward the back, close to the kitchen, and I will be at the stove early in the morning, whatever else the day may hold."

The voices of the two girls could be heard even before they opened the door – mainly Annie's voice, but with Margaret answering her questions. Margaret was used to giving instructions, telling Michael her needs, cajoling her mother or her father into responding, all within the shelter of a small tidy home. Now she was in the midst of an adventure. Things unknown and surprising were before her. Annie led Margaret and Kathleen up one dark stairway, and then up another flight, and then another. High up in the great house, tucked under the eaves, was a row of small rooms, servants' quarters, and one of them was Annie's. Close by was the room with two beds where William had deposited Kathleen and Margaret's bags. Each room now had a flickering candle, the only light except a bit of moonlight coming through the small window. Margaret was too excited to sleep.

Sleeping and Waking

"He sleeps all the time, Ma," Michael said, as Kathleen put down her bag. She had come back to Fermoy early in the morning with Dr. Powers, as he made his weekly trip to see patients with a variety of maladies and wounds. The several days in Donaldstown had been satisfying, tasks completed, although heaven knows there was still much more to be done. She had been fearful about leaving Margaret behind; but Margaret was ready to be on her own, and service in the great house at Winston Court was the first step along the road. Going into service was not always a good thing. Life could be cruel, and promises of fair pay and protection could be simply lies. That Annie was there was a welcome distraction, when the moment came for Kathleen to leave Margaret behind. A home away from home, another home for you, Kathleen said to her: Jane Ellen and Annie will look after you, and Dr. Powers and Lady Elizabeth will see to your welfare.

For herself, it was good to be back in her own place again, with the teakettle on the stove. In a fortnight, she had agreed to go again to Donaldstown, to spend another three or four days scrubbing and bringing order into the long-neglected rooms. In the meantime, Alexander needed her attention.

It was mid-morning before Alexander was awake and dressed. The last several days had been disorienting for him, with Kathleen not in her accustomed place, and her return made things more normal once again. He had had difficulty putting his finger on what was missing: his mind drifted, as he sat beside the window. But now she was here once again, and life was as it should be.

Kathleen settled herself in her chair beside the table, with a cup of tea and a basket of mending. Alexander sat with folded hands near the window, his eyelids drooping. He had diminished, shrunken, in the few days she had been away. He smiled at her, but vaguely, as if he was looking at someone with whom he was not familiar. She reached out her hand to him, and he took it uncertainly, not sure who or what he was touching.

"Michael, I need you to go to the market, to get something for supper. A fish, a fine fish, and a bit of butter for the frying pan." She reached deep into her bag, and brought out two coins of the money she had received from Elizabeth Powers for her labors at Donaldstown, and gave it to her son. A fish might revive Alexander a bit, remind him of the things he loved most. She would see.

Alexander looked again at Kathleen. "I would like to be fishing again. The fish are in the river, I am sure, and it is a lovely place to be. Perhaps tomorrow."

Michael came in through the door, with a fish, wrapped in newspaper, in his hands. "Here is the fish, Ma. They are recruiting for the war: I want to go, Ma. I can sail the seas, and see the world. It is too long I have been here in Fermoy. If I go, then you and Da can live your own lives, not think about me."

Kathleen took the skillet, and put the butter in it, and cooked the fish, first on one side and then the other. "Your Uncle John has promised you a calf, and he needs your help." She paused. She knew that Alexander was beyond saying much of what was in his mind. It was the impending war, she thought, that had broken off his engagement with the world around him. She did not want to see Michael move on, into the same ritual game, of bludgeoning strangers into an alien soil. "John promised you a calf, son, and he will be hard pressed to run the farm without you." Uniforms, how she hated them, she thought. If Michael left, if Margaret had a new life, if Alexander died – what then of her? She felt again the desperation of years ago, and the loss of Brendan.

Michael was tall, gangly, not a child. Inside the house, he felt trapped, ready to explode. Not that he had any love of the sea, or thirst to do battle; but he must escape. He must go, whatever it meant to those around him. Wordlessly, he went out the door, into the dusk. If he stayed here, in

Fermoy, he would be one more builder of stone walls, breaking rocks into pieces, lifting them into place, making barriers to keep the likes of him out of other people's property. If he flew with the wild geese, off into the British army, he would have adventure, perhaps, but never a place to call home. If he went to work for Uncle John, at least he would have a calf of his very own.

Kathleen could never think about her brother John without seeing him with a cow. John delighted in livestock fairs, not because of the crowds and the gaiety and food and drink, but because of the large quiet animals gazing curiously at the passersby. It was not the horses that drew him, but the cows, with their enormous liquid eyes and their fulsome bodies. He drew great pleasure from walking among them, laying a hand on their backs or flanks, knowing that they would stand calmly and neither flinch nor withdraw from his touch.

He had visited Kate in Fermoy the year before, when he was on his way to one more fair, this time not just to look wistfully at the cows but to buy one and take it home to the farm. A cow could turn the fallow fields into milk and butter: that was the sensible reason for his search. But there was something more. A cow would be a companion, a helpmate, in his life's work, uncomplaining and supportive and trusting on good days as well as bad.

The land along the Blackwater was rich with fine dairy farms, and John was confident that his search would be rewarded. He did not much care about whether the animal he selected had won prizes, or could claim any particular pedigree. The animal would bring completeness and fulfillment into his life. It would respond to his touch, willingly, when he milked it, and give forth a flow of rich liquid steaming in the cool morning air.

The beasts were lined up in the sunshine around the town square, most of them tethered to their owners' wagons or to the hitching posts nearer to the fountain. John looked carefully at each one, striving not to appear too excited about what he knew was a turning-point in his life. The perfect one for him would be calm, docile, not necessarily a great beauty, but his to have and to hold.

"This one here. Is she healthy?"

The owner was surprised at the one he was asking about: he had not even been sure that he would be able to sell her at all, with so many more impressive cows being shown, some of them his own.

"She's a good one, pleasant tempered, with a steady yield." What more could he say? Soft brown, not much of a sense of herself but willing to graze placidly at the edge of the field. He had only brought her to market as an afterthought, and here it seemed she might be the first one sold.

John made the circuit along the line of livestock one more time, slowly, and then returned again. "How much would you be asking for her? She might be suitable for my needs."

There was some small conversation, quickly resolved, and John took the tether and led her forth. They had a journey before them, and it was already approaching mid-day. The weather was fine, and they would have time to get acquainted, to become familiar with each other's pace and personality. "Tara." He tried out the sound of the name, as they passed out of the edge of the town. "That's my girl. Come along now."

When John had appeared at her door for the second time in as many days, Kate tried not to show her surprise; but the presence of the cow made it seem understandable, as if his journey had all been carefully planned. And then he went on home with Tara his new love, back to the farm where the chickens pecked in the front yard and his wife barely tolerated his existence, with a new companion to bring him happiness.

The night wind was moist, with the promise of rain before another hour passed. Life on a farm was as far from battlefields and garrisons as anything could be. Michael was torn between the thrill of adventure and the placid life of fields and cows. He looked up once more at the garrison walls, still unfinished, and turned back again toward the door of the house.

All in a Circle, All in a Row

During the years while Sir Hubert was living in Donaldstown, the estate had gone through a transformation. The ruin of a Norman tower, stone walls without even a roof overhead, had become the core of a great manor house. Sir Hubert had given it a name, Winston Court, and had built not just the house but walled formal gardens and carriage barns and horse barns, cottages for the house servants and for those who cared for the race horses and maintained the estate. As his fortunes and his health declined, things slid downhill, and after he died neglect took its toll on everything.

Now that Dr. George Powers was in charge, he had much simpler needs, and as the months passed he struggled to choose what must be done and what could continue to be neglected. There were rooms that could be closed off and left for some future owner to bring back to usefulness. Tenants had been found for the cottages, and they had hired enough of a small staff to meet their needs. A half dozen horses, lovely animals, still grazed in the fields. They were all of fine stock, and demanded attention. Two local men who had worked for Sir Hubert continued to deal with the horses, feeding and grooming and exercising them and seeing that they were properly shod. George Powers found the name "Winston Court" to be a silly pretension: this was no court, in his eyes, but just an unreasonably big country house.

As the household became more settled in the place, a pleasant routine was developing. He spent two days every week seeing patients in Fermoy, and he returned to Dublin every month or two to consult with colleagues and visit libraries and browse in the bookstores close to Trinity College.

Each trip would result in him returning with one more box of books, and the box would be set down with the several dozen other boxes that already were stacked in the tower room, which was destined to be his library and study. All that was required was the time and energy to take each of the hundreds of books out of their boxes, and dust them off, and arrange them on the yards and yards of empty shelves waiting for them to take up residence.

The girl Margaret seemed to have become part of the household staff quite happily. He had been uncertain what would come of it, when Mrs. Hickey agreed to let her stay for a time to see whether she had the skills and the temperament to be in service. She was literate, which was somewhat unusual, and she learned new tasks readily; and with her coming the other girl Annie was less lonely, less at loose ends and less likely to fall into troublous predicaments. He was unsure what would happen with Margaret's parents, but he suspected that Captain Hickey did not have many months of life left to him. If Margaret became more experienced and capable, it was less likely that she would soon become just a penniless orphan.

Margaret's routine at the great house had fallen into a pattern. One morning, Jane Ellen placed bread and butter and an egg in front of Margaret as she sat down in the kitchen for her early breakfast. Annie was already eating; she had been out to gather the eggs from the chickens, and her cheeks were flushed from the chill morning air.

"Lady Elizabeth wishes you to clean the new bookshelves in the tower room, so that Dr. Powers' books can be unpacked and organized," Jane Ellen said to Margaret. "I have laid a fire in the hearth there, to take the dampness out of the air. Stone walls hold the cold, and it takes some time to make a room like that warm and comfortable."

"There are ghosts and banshees in the tower," Annie said. "I've heard them moaning."

"Nonsense," said Jane Ellen. "The wind in the chimney fires up your imagination, that's all it is. Pay no attention to her, Margaret. Once you have finished cleaning and polishing the shelves, we'll see what is to happen next."

"Maggie," said Annie, "Before tea I shall take you up through the fields to see the stone circle. That's where the fairies come to dance in the moonlight. I have never been there by moonlight, but I know it's true. William told me. Aunt Jane, can we take a lump of sugar for Sir Harry when we go?"

Margaret listened, quiet, wide-eyed. She knew there were no such things as ghosts or banshees or fairies, but she loved Annie, always talking and a constant source of astonishment. She would follow her to the stone circle; she would follow her anywhere, if the truth were to be told. And in the meantime, she would polish the shelves, and unpack book after book after book.

She went to the tower room from the kitchen, carrying clean rags and a container of beeswax to lay a polish on the woodwork. The shelves were so new that they still had remnants of sawdust left by the carpenters. All of that must be removed, and then the wax applied and rubbed until it gleamed. She loved seeing the warm brown of the chestnut shelves take on a glow as she buffed the wood. So beautiful: someday she would have bookshelves, too.

It was mid-afternoon when Lady Elizabeth came to check on her progress. The tower room was sparsely furnished; it had not yet really been put to use, but once the books were unpacked, she knew that George would be spending much of his time there. The room needed a carpet, and more comfortable places to sit than the single straight-backed chair that stood before the heavy plank table that would serve as his desk. It was not a room that she would choose to spend much time in, but she knew that her husband would be there more than anywhere else.

The ladder stood in the corner, where the high bookshelves intersected, but the girl Margaret was now sitting on a wooden crate, rubbing at the surfaces of the lowest shelves. She stood up quickly as Lady Elizabeth entered the room, not wanting to give any impression of disrespect.

"You are making fine progress, Margaret. I am so happy seeing this room begin to be usable. As soon as the shelves are clean and ready, I would like you to start unpacking and organizing the books. Dr. Powers will have some instructions before you begin; I think he will be able to spend some time with you in the morning." She paused, unsure how to go on with more momentous news. "When he returned from town, he brought the sad word that your father Captain Hickey had died in the night last night. It was not completely unexpected, my dear, but it is a great loss I am sure for you and your mother." Margaret sat down suddenly on the crate; she felt faint and dizzy, for nothing had been said about this before, only intimations that things were changing, without the word "death" ever being spoken. Lady Elizabeth went on: "Your mother will be coming here in a few days, after affairs have been put in order. In the meantime, this is your home, and perhaps it can continue to be so." She laid her hand on the girl's shoulder, uncertain that her touch would be welcome but not knowing what else to do. After a few minutes she turned and left, and went back to her sitting-room and rang for Jane Ellen, who would know better what should be done, what was customary. Little that she could think of would be of use. She picked up the needlework beside her chair, something more measured and predictable and soothing, less unsettling than the turmoil of human emotions. She threaded yarn through the needle, and carefully started to add a series of stitches to the pattern on the cloth: one, two, three, four.

Margaret continued cleaning and waxing the shelves until the afternoon ended, although her mind was elsewhere. When she went down to the kitchen, and to the basin at the back to wash the wax residue off her hands, Jane Ellen was soon beside her.

"It is very sad news about your father, Margaret. He is now in a better place, but it is a great loss for you and your mother, I am sure." Margaret nodded mutely, unable to find words or even to weep tears. "When Annie comes in, why don't you go out and walk with her for a bit? It is a lovely day, and tea will not be ready yet." And, Jane Ellen thought to herself, Annie knows well this kind of loss.

The clouds in the western sky were streaked with blue and violet, and the rays of the setting sun cast a warm gold on the stone walls and the hedges along the borders of the fields. Annie and Margaret walked hand in hand, uphill along the cow-path, and then into a high field where the grass had not yet been grazed nor the hay mown. They pushed their way through the damp pasture, picking at the wildflowers along the way, and then suddenly were at the ring of stones, spaced as if to be seats for some gathering of a dozen or more dignitaries, coming together to gaze down the hillside, or to chant and dance through some forgotten ritual.

"I sit here and watch the fairies," Annie said. "Ever since my ma died, it has been the thing that made me know I was not alone. They come here and dance, and then they go back and dance with her." The girls sat on the stones, well separated from each other, both of them looking westward as the sun slipped beyond the far hill.

As the shadows lengthened and light failed, the two walked back down the cow-path. Halfway along, behind a length of fencing, Sir Henry stood grazing thoughtfully. Annie reached into her pocket and produced a lump of sugar, and handed it to Margaret. "You can give it to him," she said generously. "He loves sugar."

Margaret reached across the fence timidly, and the horse gravely took her gift. She withdrew her hand, and he extended his neck and nuzzled against her hair and shoulder. He knew he had a new friend.

Margaret was sitting on the wooden crate, waiting expectantly, when Dr. George Powers entered the tower room the next morning. He had two books in his hands, books that he had carried to his bedroom the night before, to assure that he would have something to occupy himself if he awakened before dawn.

"Good morning, Margaret," he said as she rose and curtseyed. "You have done a fine job of preparing the bookshelves. Now the real work must begin." He sat in the chair at the large table, and pulled one of the boxes of books toward him. "Books are my real treasure, you see, just as my wife's garden is for her, and Lady Amelia's chinaware and glass for her. Several tasks must be completed before things will be in good order, so that I can make proper use of my study." He opened the box. "Each volume must be inspected, to see if it has any damage that needs repair. See, for instance, that this binding is loose, and requires mending. Let us start a pile here," as he placed it at the far corner of the table, "And then I can determine what needs to be done."

He lifted the rest of the books out of the first box. "I try to limit myself to acquiring books on just a few subjects. First, of course, is medicine: more works will deal with that topic than any other. Then, agriculture and animal husbandry – some of these belonged to Sir Hubert before me, and I will have to determine how many of these are of interest to me. The ones on horses, I am sure, and probably those on botany and plant cultivation and forestry as well. A number of volumes of poetry, and philosophy; some travel books on distant parts of the Empire." He paused and looked around at the shelves. "I think that you can begin to sort them by subject, placing ten to twenty volumes on a shelf, so that no shelf is more than half full – medicine along that wall, poetry and philosophy here by the window, agriculture over there on the right. After you have unpacked and dusted the volumes, and placed them on the shelves, I will begin to rearrange them so that I can find things readily when I want them." He looked around the room again. "Do you have any questions?"

Margaret had been listening attentively, but there were other things on her mind beside the arranging of a library. "Can you tell me, please, Dr. Powers, why did my father die?" She was startled at her own boldness, but she had to know things that had not been told to her,

Kathleen Hickey had asked the same question of him, just a day earlier. "Death comes in many ways," he said gently. "Sometimes by sickness; sometimes by accident or tragedy. Sometimes it is simply that the length of a life has run out, and that is the gentlest passing, though the most difficult to explain. All my books on medicine can tell me very little about it." He looked at Margaret as she stood before him. "Perhaps you will have a better understanding of these things some day than I have." The girl had an air of sadness, but also of curiosity: she needed to understand what had happened, not just recover from the shock. She has the makings of an interesting woman, he thought to himself, someone willing to risk exploring things in new ways as she grew older. She was someone who was able to learn, perhaps even from books: he liked to see that.

"Where did all of these books come from? I did not know there were this many books in the whole world." When she had lived at home, her father had had a prayer book, and a Bible, and several volumes with plans and diagrams of fortresses and military barracks. When she had sat with her father and read from the pages of the prayer book, it had been part of the bond between them, something that they shared which had little to do with the words on the page. She was intrigued with the thought of sitting and reading to herself: who would listen, and where would all the words go once they had been read?

Dr. Powers gazed at the growing pile on the table. "Some of them belonged to my uncle Lord Hubert, and others to my father, Duncan Powers. He traveled widely, and he loved books about distant places, stories of exploration and adventure. Many of the medical books are my textbooks from when I was in school." He picked up a leather-bound slim volume, opened it and looked at the lines on the pages. "When I go to Dublin I search for volumes of poetry, like this one, and bring them home, so that I can see the world through someone else's eyes." He had not said these things before, even to Elizabeth.

"May I – sometimes after I have finished my work for the day – read in some of your books too?" She was surprised at her own forwardness, and she was not even sure she would understand the words on the pages.

Dr. Powers did not answer immediately. When he thought about where he was most at home, it was not in a building but amidst his piles of books, where his mind could wander from room to room through the different subjects of his interests. A preoccupation had been the pointlessness of having accumulated all this treasury when there was no one to share it with, no child to dive into the exploration of the unknown by opening one book after another, finding in each an unexpected universe. "Of course you may, Margaret," he said at last. "It will put all of these to good use. Just be sure to let Jane Ellen know where you are when you are reading here, in case she has need of you."

"George, I am unwell." Dr. Powers looked up, although not with alarm, as Lady Amelia entered the room. His conversations with his mother frequently started with these words. The two of them did not have many interests in common, and her symptoms, real or imaginary, gave them something to talk about. His father Duncan Powers would have preferred a son who chose to become a merchant, to follow his own involvement in importing goods from the Orient, spices and tea and silks and jewels.

The discussion about books between the doctor and Margaret was not finished, but it was interrupted. Lady Amelia stood between the two, facing her son and ignoring the girl. "I am chilled, George, and my bones are aching; the dampness here is more than I can bear." He rose from his chair and put his arm around her shoulder to soothe her.

"You would feel better in your sitting room, or with Elizabeth; those rooms are warmer than it is in here. And a cup of tea will warm you; let me call Jane Ellen and have her bring it to you." He eased his mother toward the door. Her dress, lovely though it was, needed at least a shawl around her shoulders to make her comfortable. But that was not the point, he knew: she was lonely, and her own idleness bothered her, but she did not know how to remedy it. George and Elizabeth were habitually busy, and she took it as a reproach that they would not stop what they were doing and devote themselves to providing her with companionship and their undivided attention. For now, for a little while, he was with her.

Margaret, abandoned, remained in the tower room, sitting on the wooden crate. She was alone, but with work to do, and she went on with the books – lifting each one from the box where it had been packed, dusting and inspecting each volume, and then placing it in its appropriate place on the table or on the shelves. And then, after a while – there was no reason not to – opening a book, turning the pages, acting as if it were her very own. It was a large, old book, and the leather binding was engraved with gold letters: <u>Markham's Masterpiece, Touching the Curing of All Diseases of Horses.</u> It was written not for a simple household servant, but for the people who owned and cared for the great beasts. She tried to imagine that Sir Harry was *her* horse, and that *she* had to decide about shoeing the great animal, grooming him, seeing that he was exercised and sheltered and cared for. She leafed through the pages, looked at the illustrations, finely drawn plates of beautiful horses, and then closed the book and gazed out the window. Fields and trees beyond, polished woodwork, shining parquet floors, high stone walls.

The Placement of Treasures

Amelia had always had a sense of certitude about the things that were important to her. The shape, the color of a porcelain bowl or vase; the clarity of a crystal decanter. In London, every surface in the Powers house had been used to display her treasures. The decoration on a jar or platter could absorb her attention for days: there was something much more permanent about it than the distraction of people and mindless conversation.

She did not yet feel really settled at Donaldstown, although she had resigned herself that this was the place where she was likely to spend the rest of her mortal days. Some parts of the great house she had not yet even seen, but the two rooms that were truly hers – a bed chamber and a sitting room – were now becoming comfortable and pleasant, with walls painted the color of honey, and furnishings on which her favorite things could be placed, so that once again she could admire them, meditate upon them, recall the occasion when each one had come into her possession.

She could read these artifacts as if they recounted the story of her life – particularly of her life with Duncan, and the times when he was away on distant voyages and the things he had to tell her when he returned. He would talk of markets and bazaars, of festivals and temples and ceremonies, but her fascination was not with these ephemeral places and events, but with the solid definable perfect objects that he brought back, unwrapping each one of them carefully as he talked to her, giving a detailed description of a place that she listened to not at all. She concentrated her gaze on what was in the package, savored it, touched it gently and respectfully, and then placed it on a table or a cabinet shelf. He brought jewelry, studded with emeralds and rubies, and she kept these carefully in their boxes; but they did not have the same resonance as the objects she really loved. The jewels were just baubles, and could provide a momentary splendor. She barely remembered that she possessed them, and would happily give them away; but Elizabeth would not have loved them either.

The ivory brooch was different from the other jewelry. She wore it much of the time, although it was simple, with delicate carving, something small and of exquisite delicacy. It had come, Duncan told her, from Siam, and the flower engraved on it – a lotus blossom – was more than just a thing of beauty; it also had a spiritual symbolism in the land where it was made. She did not care about that. She loved its oval shape, and often she would raise her hand to it and run her fingers over the curved indentations on its surface. Sometimes she wore it at the base of her throat, on a lace collar. On other occasions she would pin it so it held in place the shawl draped around her shoulders. The brooch was nothing ostentatious; it would barely be noticed by someone looking at her. For herself, it was her talisman of memory, of all her years of life with Duncan.

Hubert Winston, not Duncan, was the one who first appeared in her parents' parlor, when Amelia was young and in the bloom of her beauty. He must have her, he must have her; he must have her portrait painted, golden hair piled high, wearing a silken gown, a fine hunting dog lying at her feet. He came again and again, his round face beaming, his ruffled shirt front bursting forth from velvet waistcoat. She watched wide-eyed as he sat at the family dinner-table devouring serving after serving of beef roast, gazing amorously across the table as he chewed. And then he would sit beside her in the parlor after dinner, trying to contain his infatuation, telling her of his enormous mansion in Ireland, and of the place of honor in the great hall where her portrait would hang, and of how much he cared for her. She sat with her hands primly folded and her eyes lowered. Her only feeling toward Winston was aversion: she wished to recoil from his presence.

When his cousin Duncan returned from the East, Hubert Winston brought him to dinner as well, further proof to Amelia's parents that his life of horses and hounds had some substance behind it. Duncan was thin, recovering from the ravages of some tropical fever, and dressed with the oddity of someone who had long been traveling and was therefore out of step with the fashions of the day. He had an air of preoccupation, as if his mind was still continents away from where his body now found itself. But he listened attentively to his host, and to his cousin Hubert's bombastic meanderings. And, as they said farewell at the end of the evening, he gave Amelia a small box – just a trinket, he said, in thanks for the pleasant hospitality. Inside the carved wooden box was an ivory brooch.

Amelia, she of the long golden hair, the primly folded hands, decided to enter into a conspiracy – first only with herself, then with her parents as well. She could not leave London, that was clear to her: her parents needed her presence, and she would be sacrificing the things she must do if she left for a distant Irish estate, endowed though it might be with gardens and horses and elegant chambers. She would stay here, close to home, where her parents needed her, and where Hubert might occasionally visit. And Duncan as well, when he returned from his travels, his voyages to the East, his business interests in distant places.

Hubert's entreaties – the great house, the horses, the hounds; the place reserved for her portrait, opposite the stairway with its carved rail – were to no avail. It was here, in London, close to the Thames, where her parents were, where she was needed, where she belonged. He would always be welcome at their table, Amelia's father assured Winston; but as a guest, only that.

Duncan also went away; but then he came again, months later, this time bringing a small vase of celadon porcelain, moss-green and quiet and serene. She held it and ran her fingers over its smoothness, and placed it atop a table near the parlor window, and every day she cut a fresh rose and put it in the vase.

Duncan first sailed to the Eastern seas as a young man, dutifully pursuing a livelihood in the spice trade, with only a faint hope that the livelihood might become a fortune. He learned the skills in bargaining which were needed to buy cotton in Madras, and then spices in the tropical islands that straddled the Equator. And then he moved on to Canton, to the tea trade, where it was almost routine to become wealthy. Every few years he would return to England, partly to put his fortune to good use, partly to recover his health after suffering the maladies and fevers of trop-ical ports and months at sea. The tea chests that he bought in Canton, filled with tiny dark dry leaves, became the building-blocks of his for-tune, as they were sold in the demanding market for tea in the British Isles. As a diversion, he bought other things on his journeys to the East, things that could be stored and carried in much smaller boxes – bronze bowls, celadon vases, gold or ivory brooches. Once he had met Amelia, he recognized the value of this pastime.

They were married quietly, and settled in a lovely London town house just a short distance from where her parents lived. He stayed for several months in London, enjoying domesticity and improving his standing among the shareholders of the East India Company, and then he left again on one of the great sailing ships heading for the East. Four months after his departure, George was born, their first and only child. The boy would be almost four years old before he met his father, this time return-ing not just with tea chests and carefully-wrapped porcelain, but with wooden toys, carved elephants and tigers and monkeys, a compensation for the missing father whom George scarcely knew he had.

The tea trade was the great obsession of Englishmen like Duncan, who sought to become wealthy. Tea chests, the large wooden boxes packed with varieties of the dried leaves, were carefully protected on the long sea voyage, piled on top of other smaller boxes containing porcelain – chi-naware, as it was called – which was less susceptible to the dampness of decks and holds awash with ocean spray. However long his stay in foreign ports might be, Duncan would reserve the last few days before sailing for home for a personal journey of exploration and discovery, seeking out a length or two of fine silk, a bowl of bronze or silver or gold, an object of carved jade of creamy moss-green hue. He had come to the understand-ing that these things communicated more than words did with his lovely serene wife, waiting at home with his young son George who seemed to double in size between his infrequent return trips from the other side of the world. And, each time, his growing prosperity would be safely depos-ited so there would be no danger of his wife and child being left indigent if he did not return. So many never returned, of those who sailed east seeking treasures.

George knew the beautiful objects were to be looked at, not touched, from the time when he was too small even to reach up to them. As he grew, he was soon tall enough to look straight on at them, but that was not where he directed his gaze. Instead, he stood at the window, looking at the world outside, people and horses and carriages passing by. He loved people, and wished that he could be part of the activity and turmoil of the world, not just enclosed inside with his mother and the household staff and his tutor Hendrik. Amelia imagined that George was watching for the return of his father, not that he was contemplating an escape route, a pathway that would allow him to become part of humanity, not just an object to be gazed upon.

Duncan was in London for several months at the time when George turned sixteen. Old enough, the father thought, to take on the preparation for a career, whatever it might be – something in the world of commerce, he hoped. But his son already had another plan: he would wish first to attend university, and then undertake the practical study to become a physician, in Dublin or Edinburgh, not so far away, but far enough to become his own person, to make friends, to walk arm in arm with someone while absorbed in conversation, not just to stand alone and contemplate bronze bowls and porcelain dinnerware. He was adamant; his father relented. A physician might never be prosperous, but there was some utility in what he sought to do. He could establish himself in a place, and do some good for humankind. And he would be able to care for Amelia, George's mother, Duncan's wife, should the need arise.

A Household of Substance

"There you are, Margaret." Kathleen appeared at the door of Dr. Powers' study, her shawl still around her shoulders after the trip from Fermoy.

Margaret looked up, startled, from the pile of books beside her on the floor. "Oh, Ma, I thought you had forgotten me entirely." She put down the rag she had been using to clean the dusty volumes, and wiped her hands against her skirt as she stood up. "I have felt so strange without you here."

Kathleen Hickey put out her arms. "See, you have grown taller in just three weeks. So much has changed, so suddenly. I missed you every day, but it gave me heart, knowing that you were safe and warm here." She pulled her shawl off and folded it, clasping it with her arm. "I told Jane Ellen that I must see you before I set to work. We will be together again at the table, but now I must go and see what tasks she has for me." She put her hands on her daughter's shoulders, reassuringly, and looked out the window at the rain falling on the fields beyond. "Life is never perfect, Maggie, but there are good things in every day, if you just look for them."

Margaret nodded, and turned again to the bookshelves. In the weeks since her mother had left, she had felt incomplete, abandoned. Now very little had changed, but a certain balance had returned in her life. She lifted a stack of books and placed them on the shelves, each one carefully inserted in its assigned place.

Kathleen went first to get her instructions from Jane Ellen in the kitchen. Then she went once again to the great hall, dark and gloomy with its portraits glaring down at her, but this time familiar like an old friend. She carried the ladder, and the feather duster and rags, but a burden was lifted from her shoulders, now that she had seen Margaret here in a proper place, where she was both safe and exposed to new possibilities. She looked again at the paintings on the walls: horses, dogs, castles; ladies and gentlemen in elegant dress. They were intimidating as they stared down at her from on high. But once she climbed the ladder, looked at them eye to eye, they seemed less pretentious, even a bit silly, perhaps, in their foppish and overly-ornamental costumes. Lady Elizabeth and Dr. Powers and Lady Amelia did not put on such airs, she thought to herself, as she rubbed at the frames to remove the dust and grime.

The picture frames were elaborate, with rosettes and curlicues several inches wide and deep, and she threw herself into the task of scrubbing, vigorously but carefully enough that the gilding did not come off with the dirt. She stared back at the faces in the portraits, eye to eye with personages who would not have acknowledged her if she appeared before them. This is my world, she said to each of them; you only peer at me from afar, watching my daughter as she walks before you, growing day by day. Just decorations, she told herself; nothing of their pretensions can injure Margaret. She has the strength to stand on her own.

The next morning Lady Elizabeth sent for her, after breakfast and before she began the day's tasks. "Margaret is a good girl, Kathleen, and we will be happy to have her on the household staff. Jane Ellen will see to her well-being, and you are near enough that she can see you occasionally."

"I plan to move with my son to my brother's farm, mum, and we will still be not too far away. I know she will be diligent and work hard to please you, milady." Kathleen blinked her eyes, not wishing to be seen with tears on her cheeks; she raised the corner of her apron to her face, rubbed quickly, and lowered it again. Lady Elizabeth stood up from her chair, and Kathleen curtseyed before she went down once again to the kitchen.

The kettle was steaming, and Jane Ellen sat at the table, with long rows of silver serving-forks and spoons, ladles and tureens and gravy boats, laid out before her awaiting a vigorous polishing. She always took great satisfaction in polishing silver: it was a reminder that she was employed in a household of substance, even though much of the silverware was rarely put to use. "A cup of tea, Kathleen: serve yourself and sit for a bit, before you go on to the next task." She could sense Kathleen's mood, a mixture of relief and determination and sadness. So hard to think about cutting a child loose from yourself, placing her in God's hands, with little more that you can do for her.

George Powers awakened in the morning to look out on the meadows, to hear birdsong at the sunrise. He was absorbed in this new life in the south of Ireland, so different from Dublin's streets and clinics and epidemics. The city's tenements and and sick poor were fading from his thoughts. He had loved the turmoil, the challenge, of being a physician surrounded by urban ills, where there was always work to be done, a new crisis every day. But that was why most of his books had spent years packed in boxes, waiting for a time of leisure when he could rediscover them once again.

The grand double staircase in the great hall had a small pocket door partway up, which led into his study in the tower. From inside the room, the door was hardly visible: it matched the paneling of the walls, and when opened it slid almost soundlessly behind the adjacent panel. When he returned from Fermoy, or from other visitations to the sick in the surrounding countryside, he would climb the stairs and open the pocket door, entering a different world. Today had been such a day, and an afternoon of reading and writing letters as the sun set beyond the western window would relieve his mind.

"Ah, Margaret. Reading again!" He smiled as he stepped through the door.

Margaret scrambled to her feet, startled at his sudden appearance. "Yes, sir. Three more boxes are unpacked today, and almost all of them are in fine condition. This volume here, though – the cover is almost completely off it. Most of them are in French or Latin, so I am not sure I have placed them properly." She rubbed her hands against her apron.

She handed the damaged book to him, and he turned it over and examined the stitching before he laid it on the desk. "Some like this are almost too far gone to save. What was the volume that you were reading?"

She lifted it off the shelf – a manual of human physiology, with plates and diagrams of muscles and organs. "I should not have been wasting time, sir, but it is so interesting to see what is known, how a person's body holds together. What a marvel it is." She looked down at the pages open before her. "I wish someday I could know about all these things."

He gave the girl an appraising glance. "Perhaps you will, Margaret. In Dublin, the great hospitals are more and more the domain of women who are trained as nurses, who are as important in the care of the sick as the physicians. Indeed, the nurses are with the patients all day and all night, and many owe their lives to them." He walked across the room and sat down at his desk. "For now, though, the work at hand is to bring some order out of this chaos, and you are doing well at the task." He pulled a pile of stationery out if its box. "I have some letters to write, and I am sure that Jane Ellen has some other tasks for you this afternoon. The books can wait for tomorrow."

* * *

"The girl Margaret is very promising," George Powers remarked to Elizabeth as they sat together at dusk. "She has the makings of more than just a cleaning woman. She learns quickly and has an inquiring mind. Soon the task with the books will be finished. There must be other things she could learn to do in the household."

"Perhaps," murmured Elizabeth, "She could be of aid to your mother." It was much on her mind that Lady Amelia was still adrift in a world where she did not want to be, and Elizabeth had no other world to offer her. "This is a lonely place for her in her old age. And Margaret is a bright girl, but unschooled, so there is much she has yet to learn. Your mother could guide her, help her become more useful."

The quiet returned as darkness gathered. George was remembering his own youth, his mother gazing at her treasures, leaving him to the direction of others in the household, of visits to his grandparents. He did not know whether she would do more than that for a stranger, an Irish girl.

In the morning he ventured into his mother's sitting room. Her hands were folded in her lap. Her stillness where she sat made her seem almost invisible - a wraith, with her shawl blending into the back of the upholstered sofa. No energy flowed forth from her; she was barely there.

"Mother," George began, "Soon the girl Margaret will have finished shelving the books in my study, and I would like her to begin taking over the task of helping you, cleaning and dusting your rooms and giving you whatever assistance you need." He paused. "She is a pleasant girl, quite promising. She can read, but she has no schooling beyond what her father gave her. She has much to learn."

Lady Amelia listened, but did not respond for several minutes. Her mind seemed to be elsewhere. "Do you remember a box," she said at last, "Black, and inlaid with mother of pearl, that I always kept on my desk? In it I kept a pen, and the keys to the desk drawers, and it was beside the ink-well. Since I came here I have not seen it." She looked up at him, almost a glance of accusation. He could not recall what she was talking about: when last he had lived in her house, his preoccupation had been outside the windows, not the objects and trinkets on her desk.

"I have no recollection of it. There are still many boxes stored away: it must be hidden in one of them. If Margaret could help you to sort through things, I am sure it will appear."

She lifted one hand to the ivory brooch, and then returned to the stillness of her folded hands. "This girl, Margaret, how do you know she is to be trusted? She has no breeding, no education. George, you and Elizabeth move too quickly to take on the world's burdens. You may regret the day she came here. A simple Irish girl."

He stood up abruptly. "We can talk more about this later." Argumentation would accomplish nothing. "Her father, you know, was an honorable man, as English as you or me, an officer in His Majesty's Army who comported himself well in the American colonies and then here in Ireland. True, her mother is Irish, but a good-hearted and decent woman. We all have times of misfortune in our lives." It was rare that he had spoken to his mother in this fashion: she was always of pale complexion, but now she was paler, her lips tight, her folded hands clasping each other rigidly. He turned and left the room, closing the door gently but firmly behind him.

Sustenance

The kitchen's warm steamy air was sustenance. Sunlight streamed through the windows, and the teakettle rattled on the stove. Jane Ellen stood kneading bread, her strong arms folding vigor into the staff of life. Annie sat with a bowl of porridge and a cup of tea, daydreaming, her spoon suspended in mid-air, her mind out in the meadows listening for the lark's song. She barely noticed Margaret's entrance into the room, filling her cup and bowl and sitting down across from her.

"Annie, where are you?" Margaret said, startling her into wakefulness. Jane Ellen watched, amused; these two were almost daughters to her now, but so different from each other, in what they were today and were likely to become.

"I am hardly awake yet. It was so cold outside, when I went to gather in the eggs. I would like to be back in bed, under the covers: please, Jane Ellen, just this once, can't I go to sleep again?" She knew the answer. Jane Ellen did not even respond, as she put the kneaded dough back into its bowl to rise, and covered it with a towel. These two were the real people in Margaret's life. They had become her family, the ones whose caring touched her and gave her solace. Not that she was not grateful to Dr. Powers and his wife: they were most kind, but their concern was of a different sort than the friendly affection of those who she met at the kitchen table.

"William gave me a bouquet of flowers," Annie said softly. "He wants me to walk out with him this evening." Margaret looked at Annie sceptically. William, she thought, was an old man, almost twice their age. But what did that mean? More than two decades had separated her own father and mother, and she had never considered that to be awkward or improbable. But Annie was like her, still a girl, happy to wander off in search of stone circles and fairy forts when the setting sun cast its lengthening shadows.

"Still reading books, Margaret?" Jane Ellen asked. Margaret's face reddened. For the other two, fairy forts were far more real and practical than what was found between the cover of books. She could not explain to them about the adventures she had while sitting on her stool in Dr. Powers' study, her dust cloth in one hand, the other turning the pages of the book in her lap. Too soon, the books would all be shelved, and there would be no more excuse for an escape into reading.

William had replaced Margaret as Annie's companion for late afternoon walks. Left alone, Margaret had come to exploring the walled garden, watching it change as Lady Elizabeth had the weeds and overgrowth stripped away, and new rose bushes planted to climb the trellises against the brick walls. The beds spilled over with lavender and lilies now that the summer had come and the days of daffodils had past. A brick pathway circled the bed of herbs at the center of the garden. Margaret had discovered the volumes of herbals among Dr. Powers' collection of books, and each afternoon she looked for new surprises among the garden plants, leaves that could be dried for seasoning food or pounded into pastes and poultices to cure a fever or heal a bruise. Lady Elizabeth smiled indulgently when she saw the girl beside the bed of herbs. She chose her plants for their color, their sturdiness, the shape of their leaves or blossoms, but she was happy that someone else also took delight in them.

Margaret was kneeling, her head buried in a wild thicket of mint, when Elizabeth came up behind her. "I should make you my head gardener, child. You look like you belong here."

Margaret stumbled to her feet, brushing her hands against her skirt. "I love the smells – mint, and the lavender, and rosemary and thyme. Each one is so different, and I am learning about them from the books in Dr. Powers' library."

"Tomorrow," Elizabeth said to Margaret, "I wish you to start spending every morning helping Lady Amelia. Like Dr. Powers, she also has things still to be unpacked, and she needs help with dusting and arranging her belongings in her sitting-room. She is not an early riser, so it would be best if you do whatever other work Jane Ellen has for you first, and then when Lady Amelia rings for her breakfast you can take it up to her and see what assistance she would like from you."

Margaret nodded assent, trying to look pleased at the new prospect, but feeling some uncertainty. "I will do my best, mum." Her time at Donaldstown so far had been busy but uneventful, with very little human contact aside from Jane Ellen and Annie. Dr. Powers and his wife treated her kindly, but almost as a stranger. Lady Amelia had never spoken directly to her, and she sensed that she was seen as an intruder in her domain, perhaps not at all a welcome presence. Her own father had been old, though not frail like Lady Amelia. But the distance between Margaret's age and her father's had been part of their bond, not a barrier. His hand upon her head had been more than just a sign of affection. It was part of the blood bond between them, the passing on of memories, of things shared but never spoken. She thought of her mother almost every day, but her father was fast fading from her thoughts. Now, as Lady Elizabeth talked, he was suddenly clearly once again in her mind's eye, and she could feel the weight of his hand, see the prayer-book open on his lap as she knelt beside his chair.

Early the next morning, Margaret was in the kitchen, awaiting instructions.

"Lady Amelia is quite particular. She expects her pot of tea to be hot, the pitcher of cream to be warm; her egg to be halfway between soft- and hard-boiled, and her toast to be fresh and quite warm, but not buttered. She wishes butter and jam – plum jam, if we have it – and a small bowl of sugar, with a spoon beside it. And all of this, as soon as possible after she rings for it." Jane Ellen smiled, and placed a tray on the table.

Margaret set the dishes and a clean folded napkin tidily in place. Once the bell from Lady Amelia's room rang, she assembled everything Jane Ellen had itemized, and then placed fresh warm toast on its salver, and a silver cover over it to hold the heat. Jane Ellen nodded, and Margaret picked up the tray and cautiously started her ascent of the stairs.

When she entered the sitting room, Lady Amelia was already seated at her table, and she looked critically at the tray set down before her:

something must be awry, something that would not meet her expectations. She moved the fork and knife off the napkin, felt the cream-pitcher to ascertain that it was truly warm, poured tea into the cup to see that it was adequately brewed. Everything seemed acceptable, at least marginally so. She gave a curt nod. "I shall ring again when I am ready for you to clear the tray." Margaret curtseyed and left the room: no misfortunes, at least this time.

While Lady Amelia was sitting with her tea, Elizabeth entered the room. "Good morning, mother. How are you?" She smiled, waiting for the daily itemization of complaints.

"That new girl: do you think she can be trusted, carrying a tray of your good dishes up and down stairs? These country girls are so careless and unreliable. It would be more satisfactory if I had brought servants with me from London." Lady Amelia's face spoke of disapproval tinged with resignation: this was her house, perhaps, but not her world.

"Margaret has seemed quite meticulous and attentive to detail, from what we have seen so far. George and I hope that she may stay with us for a long time, so we are seeing that she learns how to do a variety of tasks properly." Before Lady Amelia had a chance to respond, she went on, "After she has cleared away your breakfast, she will come back to help you with unpacking the things that you still have in boxes, and they can be polished and arranged so that you can enjoy them."

One of Lady Amelia's chronic complaints had been that she could not see and enjoy her treasures, the things that brought to mind her younger days. If this grievance was resolved, she would have to replace it with another.

"Can she do mending?" she inquired petulantly. "Everything I own seems to be falling apart."

"Let us start today with one thing, and see how that proceeds," Elizabeth responded. "There will be time enough for mending in the weeks ahead." Jane Ellen's life was fully occupied in the affairs of the kitchen; and Annie, the other girl, showed little promise for anything that required as much attention to detail as mending. And the truth of the matter was that companionship for Lady Amelia, however querulous and contrary she might be, was a major concern. The Irish countryside was lovely, but it was a prison of loneliness for an old lady from London.

"A servant girl should be well-mannered and docile and submissive. I do not like the look about her eyes." Lady Amelia pressed her hands on her lap, smoothing her skirt and then rubbing her fingers along the seam, signaling her sense of irritation.

"I hope that you can be helpful in training her, because we think that she will take on growing responsibility here. She learns quickly. George hopes that she will be able to help him when he does clinic visits, particularly when there are mothers and children who need to be seen. She has a good gentle touch, and her curiosity makes it easy for her to grasp and retain ideas." Elizabeth turned toward the door. "I will be in the garden for the rest of the morning, and will come for you when lunch is ready at mid-day."

The staircase leading to the kitchen was narrow, dim, quiet, except for the creaking of the wooden treads. Margaret went up and down the flight of stairs alone, but shadows playing on the wall, cast by reflected light from the hallway near the kitchen, gave her companionship, friendly figures making no demands upon her. Lady Amelia did not frighten her, though her manner might be distant and forbidding.

As she entered the kitchen Jane Ellen handed her a towel and a freshly-washed soup pot. There were always pots to be dried. Sitting quietly with folded hands was for another kind of person.

Skill With a Needle

"Your stitches are not straight and even. They must be redone." Lady Amelia took up her small pointed scissors once again, and ripped out the seam that Margaret had carefully mended, an hour of painstaking work.

Margaret kept her head lowered, not wishing to appear disrespectful. This had happened before, and it would happen again. She was not a skillful needlewoman, but she was meticulous, and her stitches would have held up to continued use for a long time.

Over the preceding weeks, Margaret and the old woman had reached a truce on the matter of the unpacking of the treasures. Not that she was trusted: Lady Amelia still watched her with a gimlet eye, almost a glare; but she did not interfere with what Margaret was doing – lifting each piece carefully, inspecting it for chips or scratches or tarnish, turning it over on her lap, then dusting and polishing it, and putting it on an appropriate surface. Wherever she placed an object, Lady Amelia would find it necessary to move it, at least a few inches, perhaps turn it slightly so a different aspect of its decoration was easily visible.

But the matter of mending was still a battleground. What Margaret knew of the skill was purely utilitarian, a way to hold something together that was on the verge of falling apart. Lady Amelia saw it as quite a different matter, a high art form, a way of disguising something that was threadbare and making it appear to be whole and substantial, even perfect, once again. And so her pursed lips, her sharp little scissors, her words of instruction and correction and reproof, continued to be part of the morning routine.

The afternoons were quite different. When the day was rainy, Jane

Ellen put Margaret to work in the kitchen, scrubbing and chopping vegetables, or turning fruit into jam. Or there were days when Dr. Powers let it be known that his books were once again in disorder, straying from their proper places on the shelves, and needed her attention. On more pleasant days, Elizabeth had garden tasks for her to attend to: weeding, removing dead blooms and leaves, cultivating the moist soil.

And then once a week – almost always on Thursdays – she would accompany Dr. Powers on a clinic visit to one of the surrounding towns and villages. When they arrived, mothers and children would be waiting, children with fevers and coughs and rashes, some of them cheerful and some of them crying, most of them needing a bath and too many with lice crawling in their hair. As they rode to the clinic in the small carriage, usually with William sitting atop in the driver's seat, Dr. Powers would instruct her in the things that must be done, the reasons that lice could lead to great damage to a child's health, the virtues of soap and clean water, the terrible scourge of smallpox and what could be done to prevent its spread.

Smallpox was like a storm cloud always looming on the horizon. Every village and town had citizens whose faces were marked by the disease they had suffered as a child, leaving them scarred and ugly though still very much alive; and every graveyard had its small stones over the remains of children, and many more burials left unmarked, where the young victims who did not survive had been laid to rest. The glimmer of hope, that now somehow the ravages of the malady could be prevented, were scoffed at by many as one more old wive's tale. But Dr. Powers was willing to risk being regarded as a fool if it could save lives, and so he began to experiment with the technique, cleaning a child's arm and then scratching it with a needle, and then rubbing a small amount of the dried scabrous material from the skin of a smallpox survivor, and then waiting to see if an illness developed and if the child recovered to normal health. It seemed to work, almost always: some children never became ill at all, and others had a time of feverishness and discomfort, and then recovered, with few if any pockmarks left behind. He trained Margaret in the inoculation process: particularly the younger children were less intimidated by the young woman than by the dignified gentleman doctor with his waistcoat and spectacles and graying side-whiskers. She was gentle with the young ones, and soothed their tears, and held them until they were smiling once again.

On the ride home, Margaret would have a stream of questions for him. Sometimes he knew the answers, and sometimes he was just as puzzled as she about why things happened in a certain way. Her curious mind was like a treasure-chest, with one prize after another tucked away to be put to some future use not yet defined. Insect bites, and fevers and maladies, and epidemics: so many things about which he had few straightforward answers.

"Were you not a woman, you would have the makings of a fine physician, Margaret," he said after one of her torrents of questions. He thought back to his days in Dublin, to the hospital wards and their head nurses, women who intimidated the visiting doctors with their sense of organization and their strength of will, sometimes bringing patients back to health when their cases seemed hopeless, other times bringing some peace and serenity to their final hours. They were not cheerful young girls like Margaret, however; some were Catholic nuns, and others widows who had thrown off their own grieving and put their energy into meeting the needs of others.

Their rides along the roads and country lanes revealed the constant changes in the seasons, hedgerows bursting into bloom and then shedding their blossoms, birds filling the sky and then whirling away as the autumn winds and rains came over the western hills. The circle of the year came and went and then came again, and Margaret sensed its spiral in her own life, each year repeating much the same but her eyes seeing it differently, the template of memory guiding what could be expected as the weeks and months passed.

One winter had come and gone, and then another, and spring once again colored the countryside. Dr. Powers had become more and more interested in the horses he saw – both in the ones belonging to him at Winston Court, and in the beautiful animals in the fields throughout the countryside. Sir Harry, the old reliable beast pulling their carriage, still held his affection, but he could not command the rapt attention of some of the great racing horses raised and bred by landowners in Tipperary and Cork and Kerry. George Powers had little concern for material possessions, but horses were a different matter.

Margaret had sat on her stool in Dr. Powers' study, reading from the books about horses lined up on the shelves. They dealt with the different breeds, their health, their care. Horses were treated as something more than animals, perhaps even more than humans, and just a little less than gods. She thought the great beasts were beautiful, but did not really understand the fascination with them. Dr. Powers had few obsessions: he was a man of cool temperament, and rarely showed any emotion about anything. So his absorption with horses was something to be tolerated and respected. He did not say much about it, but when their carriage was passing a field with several beautiful animals in it, he would call up to William to stop for a moment or two, so he could at least savor their strength and suppleness. He would break off the conversation with Margaret about sickness and health, about proper diet and cleanliness and contagion, and would look silently after the creatures out in the green meadow who stole his heart away.

His love of the horses in the fields at Winston Court was mentioned often when he talked with Elizabeth and Lady Amelia. These were his treasures, Margaret realized; he felt about them as Lady Elizabeth did about her rosebushes, and Lady Amelia her crystal and porcelain. More important to each of them, perhaps, than the people around them; more worthy of their attention and care.

Aside from his regular visits to clinics and to tend the sick, few things took Dr. Powers away from Winston Court, and his wife and his mother never left the estate. This tranquil life, with sunny days, and other days when it seemed the rain would never end, stretched on forever – March and April, May and June.

In June the early mornings were the most perfect time, Margaret thought. Everything was moist and brilliant, dewdrops on every blade of grass glinting in the sun's first rays. Collecting the eggs from the chicken-coop had become her daily task – it had been Annie's, but she loved the morning and Annie awakened only reluctantly. As she came in with her basket, Lady Elizabeth entered from the rose garden, with an armful of fresh blossoms to be arranged in vases at the pantry shelf. On this particular morning, George Powers followed soon behind her, wearing riding boots, muddy from his sunrise excursion across fields and up a lane to the crest of the hill, past the stone circle and the hedge rows and the long stone walls covered with fuschia bursting into bloom.

"A fine creature indeed, King Arthur is: beautiful and strong, and a pleasure to ride," he said to Elizabeth. "Indeed I think we should plan to go to Killarney next month, to see the races and look into the possibilities for breeding him. This is fine country for horses. We have been invited to stay through the races and the fair as well, and I am sure that you and mother would find it a welcome change from this solitary existence. Margaret will come along as well, to see to mother's needs and assure that she is comfortable."

Elizabeth did not answer immediately: she was reluctant to leave her roses, even for a day, but a change of surroundings would be something of an adventure. And there would be gardens, not just horses, to delight the eye.

Margaret overheard all this from the kitchen, as she transferred the eggs from basket to bowl. Killarney was a faraway place, in her mind, somewhere beyond the sunset; and the thought of riding all that way in a carriage with Lady Amelia, comporting herself properly before the elder woman's constant watchfulness, took some of the excitement out of the proposal. But the choice was not hers to be made; she would follow instructions.

Annie was not to be part of the expedition: she would stay in Donaldstown with Jane Ellen, collecting the eggs and milking the cow, missing out on the experience. It was not just the matter of her providing companionship for Jane Ellen. Now that Annie and William were keeping company, soon to be betrothed, it would be beyond the bounds of propriety for her to be part of the festivities at Blithegate, the great house where they were to visit. Dr. Powers and his wife had allowed that they could approve of Annie and William marrying, and that they could even provide some suitable accommodation for the couple on the estate once they were wed. But it would hardly be auspicious if they were thrown together prematurely: something questionable might come of it.

After Margaret had served Lady Amelia her breakfast and cleared it away, she went up to the parlor once again with a pile of completed mending, neatly folded, and waited for it to be inspected. Lady Amelia looked closely at each piece, tugging to see if the stitches would hold. Everything required close scrutiny. She refolded the pieces without any comment. This time her tiny scissors stayed on the table.

Brood Mares

Margaret adjusted the ropes securing the luggage on the back of the carriage. She could hear Lady Amelia's voice as she prepared to climb into the compartment.

"Marriage is all the girl's fit for. A cottage full of children, and boiled cabbage for every meal."

"Annie is a sweet girl, Mother dear. We cannot complain too much of her; and William will be happy to have her at his side. We could not do without William."

Dr. Powers had left two days earlier, riding King Arthur and carrying only a minimal change of clothing. He planned to stop with friends near Mallow, conferring with them about available horses and watching, if not taking part in, a fox hunt. He had no use for fox hunting, and not much for hounds either. It was the conversation – talk mainly about horses – that drew him to Mallow. All along his route, past the open fields along the Blackwater, cows and horses grazed on the green grass, lush from the rains of spring and early summer. His fields, too, must soon be dotted with horses grazing, he thought.

The carriage with the three women, driven by William, pulled by two carefully matched bays, followed a parallel route to that of Dr. Powers. The horses were selected to appear to be quite comfortable with the expedition, as if this were a customary event rather than something quite exceptional. For the week before, William's time had been spent cleaning and polishing the carriage, to conceal its long disuse, and grooming the team, talking to them and soothing them about this unaccustomed adventure. They had the makings of fine draft animals, even if they would never be suited for the steeplechase. Sir Harry was a more reluctant beast, needing coaxing and an occasional carrot to complete a journey. These two, Lord Geoffrey and Lord James, took more readily to the road.

Margaret had not ridden in such an elegant carriage before. When she had gone to the clinics with Dr. Powers, the conveyance had been a simple surrey, pulled by the docile Sir Harry. Now she sat facing Elizabeth Powers and Lady Amelia, faced with the challenge of exhibiting her best behavior – and holding her tongue – for the long day's ride.

She wanted, for one thing, to speak up in defense of Annie, her dear and cheerful friend, who had brought so much sweetness into her life. Annie was not someone with whom she could speak about nutrition and diseases and inoculation, as she did with Dr. Powers. Annie could read a bit, but only did so reluctantly, and she could not imagine how Margaret could find enjoyment sitting with a pile of dusty books in the corner of Dr. Powers' study. Her delight was in walking in the meadows, gathering wildflowers and looking for evidence of fairies along the path – evidence that she had no difficulty finding. Annie spoke to Margaret of fairy forts, and Margaret came close to believing her, however unreasonable she might know such things to be. Because of Annie, she had encountered the joy of childhood, something that it seemed had been left behind when she came to Winston Court.

As the carriage bumped and swayed along the road, bits of sunlight bounced in through the left windows, casting shadows of her folded hands on the skirt of her dress: striped fabric, gray and blue, dark enough to be suitable for traveling on a long dusty trip. Lady Elizabeth had seen to it that her wardrobe was serviceable and presentable for this rare occasion, and both the blue and gray traveling suit and a new lovely dress of dark green, very simple but striking with her light brown hair and hazel eyes, made this a memorable milestone in her life. New dresses were a rarity: being on her best behavior was part of the price to be paid.

Sitting backward in the carriage as she was, Margaret watched the receding landscape, and saw the change of shadows as the sun climbed in the sky. The two women facing her said little: the journey had started earlier in the day than Lady Amelia liked to be about, and she was closer to sleep than wakefulness once they were on the road. Both of them sat with folded hands, the picture of feminine propriety. Margaret imitated their posture. It was not something that came naturally to her. She preferred her hands to be busy, or at least holding a book before her.

By late morning the carriage came to a halt at a public house along the road, a place where the horses could be watered and the human passengers make use of a privy and then refresh themselves with tea and scones or bread, adjusting once again to standing on the firm earth after two hours of jostling. Margaret was the first to climb out of the compartment. She then extended a hand to Lady Elizabeth, and then to Lady Amelia, who was trying to awaken fully to the bustle around her. William dealt first with the horses, leading them to the trough and then back again to a fence post where he secured them and the carriage. He then disappeared through the door of the taproom, finding a place at the bar for a glass of refreshment. Margaret followed the two ladies into the tea room, unsure what was expected of her.

"Sit down with us, Margaret dear, while we have a pot of tea." Elizabeth smiled as she guided Lady Amelia to the corner table. The smell of pipe smoke and stale beer drifted in from the low door leading to the tap room. The three of them seated at the table seemed to be the only women in the building. The convivial cluster gathered at the bar, the bartender himself, and the waiter-cum-proprietor with a towel tied around his waist who came through the taproom door to their table, were all men.

"Tea, ladies? Or would you care for something stronger?"

Elizabeth ignored the effrontery of his question. "A pot of tea, and some bread and butter, if you please. The driver is caring for the horses and we have a short while to rest." She smiled tightly, not wanting to encourage familiarity with common folk, lest it make Lady Amelia uncomfortable. The sounds from the other room were cheerful, not rowdy, but she did not want to take chances, or to set a bad example for Margaret.

Without a doubt Lady Amelia would prefer to be at home, in her own parlor, all her needs taken care of and no turmoil to distract her. But George Powers had been firm: he wanted to be at this festive gathering, not just by himself, but with his family present and duly noted, so that he would be regarded with some seriousness by their hosts and the other guests, and by gentlemen who might have horses that struck his fancy. With Margaret in attendance to see to Lady Amelia's needs, everything would be quite satisfactory.

Lady Amelia fingered her ivory brooch, close to the collar of her gray traveling suit, and adjusted the shawl around her shoulders. Against her will, she was part of this expedition, taking her farther and farther from civilization. The Irish landscape was so unkempt, so unlike home. Even the cows in these fields seemed a bit disheveled. She pulled her tea-cup closer to her, stirred it with her spoon, and lifted it to her lips.

Elizabeth was looking forward to the days in Killarney with some apprehension. Her concerns were not about Lady Amelia. Margaret would deal with her needs, perhaps not to her satisfaction, but they would be adequately met. But she was not sure that she herself could ever be secure at this kind of a gathering – ball gowns, gossip, flirtations. She had no experience in this world. But in a few days it would be over, and George would be happier about his horses, and the horses that might soon be his.

The journey continued: past mid-day, into the afternoon, with one more stop for refreshment, and then more jostling along the roads leading westward. It was midsummer, and the day was long, with daylight lasting forever. The shadows were lengthening when they reached Blithegate, and theirs was one of several carriages on the long drive leading up to the great gray stone mansion, an enormous building, three or four times the size of Winston Court. As they approached the house, the pace slowed. Each carriage in turn stopped before the great front entrance, and man servants in livery opened the carriage doors, offered a hand to the passengers as they climbed down, and then untied the luggage from the back of the carriage and lined up the bags and boxes neatly beside the servants' entrance. Margaret stood to one side, uncertain what she was to do; Elizabeth and Lady Amelia were already disappearing inside the great door.

"Welcome to Blithegate, young lady. Now who would you be traveling with?" The man speaking to her was older than the others in livery, and his uniform was a bit more elaborate, although the satin collar and cuffs bore the sheen of long wear.

"The Powers family of Winston Court. Those items there are belonging to Dr. Powers and Lady Elizabeth, and the two brown ones are Lady Amelia's. And this satchel is mine," she said, picking up the smallest one.

"Just leave them all for the boys to take in; we'll see to them. Now if you step inside, someone will show you to the room where you'll be staying, and you can leave anything there before you go to assist the ladies with unpacking. Much to be done; the great dinner will be served for the gentlefolk in just an hour, and you will be joining us for supper downstairs after the dinner is cleared."

She turned obediently toward the door he had pointed out. Inside the door, the sound of laughter and many voices floated along the dark hallway. Before the journey, at Winston Court, all of the discussion had been about horses, but it was suddenly clear to her that there were many more people than horses involved in this event. She moved toward the noise and the smells of the kitchen. There was a long dining table in the wide room that opened out from the hallway, outside the kitchen itself; and near the kitchen door, a stout woman with a wide smile and a brisk, businesslike air sat at a small desk, a thick ledger book open before her.

"Your name, miss. And which party are you traveling with?"

"Margaret Hickey, mum. I came with Dr. Powers' people. I do not know if he has arrived yet."

"Welcome, Margaret. There is work to do, but time to enjoy yourself, too. Take the back stairs up to the top floor, and you will be staying in the third room on the left. Two other girls are in there as well; one of them, Grace, is on our household staff. After you have left your things, come back down, and I will have someone show you the way to where Mrs. Powers is staying. Be quick about it: I know they will want to dress for dinner, and your help will be needed."

The clanging of pots and pans sounded from the kitchen. Dinner for this large a gathering was serious business, nothing to be taken lightly. It seemed that there were a dozen people hard at work – chopping, stirring, laying out platters and tureens and serving bowls. Margaret walked toward the back stairs: up a dark staircase once again, but this time so different from her arrival at Winston Court. A festive occasion, and she was no longer a child.

Her satchel was already in the room when she reached it. Two of the beds had clothing laid out on them. She placed her bag on the third. Closing the door, she changed from her traveling suit to the green dress, hanging the other outfit on a hook on the wall. The room's small window was open, admitting a breeze. Looking out, across the rooftop and past the chimney-pots, she could see green fields, horses grazing, and the oval race track beyond.

Down the stairs once again; more long hallways, up another flight, and she was at the suite of rooms shared by Lady Amelia, Lady Elizabeth and Dr. Powers. Lady Amelia was her responsibility, and Margaret set to hanging her clothes in the wardrobe, shaking each dress to disperse the folds and wrinkles. Lady Amelia watched her closely, as if she suspected some malicious intent. Margaret had learned to endure this scrutiny, even to expect it.

When she had emptied the bags, she turned, waiting for instructions.

"Your dress is too plain, child. Come here for a moment." Margaret stepped closer, and Lady Amelia unpinned the ivory brooch from her shawl and fastened it in the center of the neckline of Margaret's dress. "I want the lavender gown laid out on the bed, that is all I will need. You can have the evening free."

People were everywhere: ladies in silk and satin gowns, gentlemen in high plumage. Below the stairs, the kitchen staff filled bowls and platters, and the servers began the procession, one course after another after another to be carried to the dining hall. Each platter went up the stairs looking like a fine oil painting, and returned like the wreckage on a battlefield. Crystal glasses and wine bottles were carried out of the kitchen on great trays, and returned in disarray. And the plates and silverware and linen, so carefully set in place, by the end of the evening were all a pile of carnage, another great work to be undertaken to bring them back to their order.

And then another table was set, the long plank dining-table in the hallway outside the kitchen, with knives and forks and plates, and bowls filled with potatoes and platters covered with sausages and slices of beef. Close to thirty people gathered round, the servants at Blithegate, and twos and threes from each of the parties visiting for the great occasion.

Margaret had never been at such a banquet; and the only person she knew by name in the whole noisy room was William. He stood leaning against the wall with two other men, one barely more than a boy and with the dark stained hands of a blacksmith, the other twice his age, but the two of them looking very much alike.

As everyone moved to the table, pulling up chairs where the places had been set, Margaret hesitated, uncertain where she belonged. William motioned to her. "Margaret, this here's Patrick Fogarty and his son Francis, who came along to see to the shoeing of the horses if that should be needed. These are people who know a lot about horses," he said with a nod and a grin, "And I think we may be seeing more of them. Patrick may have a line on two fine mares of the sort Dr. Powers is hoping to find. So you should be nice to these gentlemen, Margaret, to encourage their interest and consideration."

This was an unaccustomed occasion for her, conversation with strange men. She smiled nervously, and looked toward Francis, the younger, a fine-looking fellow despite the grime on his hands. The din around the table was sufficient that she did not feel the need to say anything. William leaned closer to her to make himself heard.

"Frank is a most competent horseman, and I think Dr. Powers may want him to ride King Arthur in the mile race tomorrow. It would be a fine chance to see what the animal can do."

Patrick and Francis knew a number of the people around them. They had been at Blithegate before, following the people who follow the horses, making their skills and experience available where it would be appreciated. The air of festivity and sociability in the room was well seasoned with the passion for horses and the excitement about tomorrow's race. Small wagers were being promised, only partly in jest; but the serious activity would wait for tomorrow.

The sound of music made itself heard through the uproar: a fine fiddle, bringing a new delight into the large room, echoing off the walls and the low ceiling. Dishes were cleared off the table, glasses and cups refilled, furniture pushed to the side, chairs rearranged around the edge of the room and in small congenial groupings. The level of noise from the voices subsided. The fiddle played on; one man began to dance, and then

another, and then men and women together; and then the floor cleared
again and Patrick Fogarty walked over to the fiddler and spoke low into
his ear. They conferred together, and both nodded and then Patrick
turned and began to sing – first a lament, in the old Irish language, and
then a song of love, with everyone quiet to the end. And then the glasses
were filled again, and once more there was revelry, and fiddler's music,
and dance.

Margaret's eyes were still on Patrick. His voice had a richness in it,
as if everything beautiful in the world flowed through the words he had
been singing. He was now talking, laughing, with others; and she sat,
with her hands folded before her, lost in the unfamiliar; and Francis,
standing with William, was gazing at her, the lovely girl in the green
dress, so quiet, so still.

"Do you like music, Margaret?" Patrick returned to the cluster of
chairs, smiling down on the young lady.

"I know nothing about music, but it is so very beautiful," she answered
softly.

"Good that you like it. I'll sing a song for you again some day," he said
with a twinkle in his eye.

William rejoined the three others, eager for more information from
Patrick. "So what can I tell Dr. Powers about these mares of yours, Patrick
Fogarty? Do they really have anything to offer?" His tone was a bit argu-
mentative, more in jest than anything. An argument was almost a necessity at a social occasion like this one; without it, an air of boredom might
set in.

Patrick filled his pipe from the pouch in his pocket, tamped it down,
tapped it against the wall beside his chair. "Perhaps you know, William,
my friend, that there are some horses in this part of Ireland whose lines go
back to the ones from Spain that came swimming to shore after the wreck
of the Armada. Not many of them, mind you, but they are quite different
from our usual breeds. The Spanish horses are a bit smaller, with a fine
build, and fast as the wind when they have occasion to run. Several of the
animals from these lines have come into my hands, and the two I have in
mind are quite ready to breed. So I could chat with the gentleman about
it, if he is interested."

Nothing more was said for a few minutes. Francis seemed to have no words at all in him. Then his father finally asked, "So what do you think of this stallion belonging to Dr. Powers. Has he got something to offer?"

The young man thought for a moment more. "Big, and powerful, no question about it. Almost too big. But I think he has the heart for the ride. We'll see on the morrow." It was more than he intended to say, at least in front of the young lady.

After the day's excitement, Margaret was suddenly weary, ready to fall asleep where she was sitting. She rose to her feet. "William, gentlemen, good night. Thank you for the lovely songs. I am sure I shall see you tomorrow." If she stayed in the room any longer she would be unable to remember the long way up the stairs to the room under the rooftop.

The stairway was dark, one flight after another, with a candle guttering inside a glass jar on each landing, just enough light to find the way. When she got to the room the other two beds were still empty; but a small oil lamp burned on the windowsill, the flame trembling with the breeze. She shed her dress and donned a shift and fell into bed, instantly asleep, dreaming not of horses and fiddlers but of a small farm yard with chickens underfoot, and a cottage with a thatch roof, and the sound of friendly conversation drifting out from the open door.

Ribbons, Ribbons

Margaret awakened to hear whispering voices. The morning light and a damp breeze came through the small window. Two girls, both younger than herself, sat together on the bed at the end of the room. She stretched, and sat up, putting her feet down to the floor.

"Awake now, are you? I'm Grace, and this here's my cousin Aileen, come down for the fair from near Tralee. I haven't seen her for a year, and we have so much to talk about. We didn't want to bother you."

"I feel like I've slept for a thousand years, and not heard a thing," said Margaret. "Perhaps it was the journey, or the excitement here last night. At home I go to bed early and wake up with the dawn."

Grace had long golden hair; Aileen had the same profile, the same blue eyes, but a head of tousled red curls atop her. They sat together like sisters, completely comfortable with each other.

"This is my first visit, though Grace has told me much about Blithegate and the horses and the fair," said Aileen.

"We both went into service at the same time, two years past now, and for all that time we haven't seen each other more than once." Grace paused, and looked at Aileen, laughing. "So there is much to tell."

"And many young men to tell about," Aileen added. "Young men, and sometimes not so young. I saw last night that you've caught the eye of Mr. Fogarty."

Margaret was not sure what to say: she was not used to talking about such things. "This was our first time meeting. Francis is a handsome fellow."

"Handsome, yes, but looks aren't enough for a man to marry on,"

Grace said. "It's Patrick Fogarty she meant: a widower, with a house and a farm, and a pleasing manner about him. Not to mention a fine voice for singing."

"Mr. Fogarty has some business with Dr. Powers, the master of my house," Margaret said defensively. "This was the first time I had met him."

"Quite convenient, Margaret, and a good piece of luck as well. Many would envy you making such a fortunate acquaintance," Grace said with a laugh.

Through the window, the ringing of distant bells could be heard, pleasant but loud enough to awaken the most determined sleeper for the festivities of the day ahead. For Grace and Margaret and Aileen, for all those who were there in service, it was a reminder of their duties: tea to be brewed, trays to be carried, dresses to be buttoned. Grace leapt to her feet, appointing herself captain of this regiment.

"Once the day is underway, and the morning tasks are done, we shall put away our aprons and go forth to the fair. Margaret, come find me in the hallway near the kitchen, and we three will go together. Be quick, now: we will have much to see and do later in the day." Each of them donned a dress appropriate to the tasks ahead, cotton but comely – Grace's a dark red, Aileen's a soft green and white check, Margaret's striped blue and gray. Margaret unpinned the ivory brooch from the green gown she had worn the night before and slipped it in her pocket, to return it to Lady Amelia. Hair combed, dresses buttoned, sashes tied, they left the room and descended the dark staircase, a small company marching downward.

Margaret donned an apron and assembled a breakfast tray in the busy kitchen to take to Lady Amelia: tea, bread, egg, butter, jam. When she arrived at the room, she rapped lightly, not wanting to awaken her, but she was greeted by a voice.

"Come in," Lady Amelia commanded. She was already in her dressing gown, seated beside a small table. Margaret laid out the breakfast, plate and cup and napkin in place, and then reached into her pocket and pulled out the ivory brooch, handing it to Lady Amelia.

"Thank you," she said. Lady Amelia responded with a slight nod of her head, even a faint glimmer of a smile.

"You must return in a half hour to assist me, and to remove the dishes. And then you will be free to enjoy the day, until it is time for me to dress for dinner." She turned to her egg and tea, as if there were no one else in the room.

In the kitchen there were always things to be done. As she entered the door Margaret was handed a towel, and pointed toward the row upon row of clean glasses, still dripping with hot water. Dry one, two, three, four, carry them to the dark wooden shelves of the pantry, line them up neatly with others of their kind – wine glasses, water goblets, large and small glasses for beer: back and forth, back and forth. By the time the glasses were dried and stored away, a half hour had passed and Lady Amelia would be ready for her assistance. Up the stairs, hold the gown for Lady Amelia, button up the back, hold the shawl until she was ready to draw it around her shoulders. Pile the dishes on the tray, give a graceful curtsey, and down to the kitchen once again. And then freedom: an adventure in a strange place, with unfamiliar faces and laughter and an unexpected surprising day unfolding before her.

As she removed Lady Amelia's dishes from the tray in the kitchen, Grace came up beside her. "No more aprons," she whispered in a conspiratorial fashion, her eyes bright. "Off to the fair. We'll meet by the outside door." She hung her apron on the row of pegs at the kitchen entrance.

The tray wiped clean, stowed in its proper cupboard, Margaret looked about her. She untied her apron and hung it on the peg next to Grace's. She took a deep breath and, decisively, walked out the door to join the others.

A day in June, with the sun shining, and a slight breeze, is something akin to paradise. Margaret, Grace and Aileen, walking the land from the gates of the great house toward the fair green, almost floated like angels, without any necessity for their feet to touch the damp grass. By this late morning hour, the serious negotiations about buying and selling horses – matters only for the men – were almost completed. For the middle of the day and the early afternoon, what remained of the fair was food and drink, tools and trinkets, linen and woolen fabrics and ribbons and laces. Not to mention gazing at the crowd, the lovely sense of being in the midst of a momentous occasion, when anything could happen and it would be no surprise.

As the three of them stood fingering the ribbons, shining in every hue, green and blue and gold and scarlet, Margaret suddenly felt eyes upon her, the same eyes as the night before.

"So, Francis, will you be racing and winning today?" She looked up at him, smiling.

"If that's what you order me to do, Miss Margaret, I will do it." He was taken aback at his own boldness. "But you must give me your order."

"And so you have it, sir. I will be standing beside the fence at the finish line." And she handed him the small green scarf that had been tucked in her pocket – an odd thing to do, but irresistible at the moment. The two other girls looked at her, awestruck.

Francis turned red, afire with sudden bashfulness and with the delight of having a young woman looking up at him, a completely unfamiliar feeling. From here he could go on to win races, circle the world, conquer the unknown. Nothing more would be necessary. He backed away, nodding his head gravely in her direction, and turned once more toward the horses lined up along the edge of the green.

Margaret looked after him. She had not really thought about what she had done – it was just an impulse - and about the impression it would make on her two companions. Something like this, a flirtation, was a new experience; it was not anything she had ever contemplated. And oh, she thought, it leads nowhere. She turned back to the table of ribbons, disguising her confusion, as she looked intently at satin and velvet, stripes and plaids. She must put her mind to other things; but the delight of the distraction of the moment stayed with her.

The two girls captured her, one at each elbow. "First, a piece of cake; and then we must go look at the horses," Grace commanded. They pulled her away, along the road with the movement of the crowd, the festive mood capturing all comers, young and old.

The long dusty lane from the edge of the village to the paddocks and the race track was crowded with people, everyone moving in the same direction as if pulled by a magnet. Gentlefolk in their finery; barefoot boys darting along the edges. Margaret and Grace and Aileen, arm in arm, drifted with the current, moving toward the track and the high wooden fence at its edge. Those in more elegant dress, ladies with their parasols, gentlemen in high hats, inspected the horses and then climbed into the grandstand, up out of the dust, to where they could see the entire great oval laid out before them, the hills beyond blue and green and violet, the sun's rays filtering through breaks in the clouds overhead. Turf accountants stood on their boxes, bulging satchels clasped under one arm, collecting wagers and writing out chits with the opposite hand, each of them with a tight knot of bettors pressing in on them. And then the great horn sounded, and the horses moved to the starting line; and the crack of the pistol and a roar from the crowd; and off with the thudding of hooves and the rising cloud of dust and one, two, three minutes of frenzy and suspense, and then with a great joyful inevitability the first horse, the great beautiful King Arthur pounded across the finish line, as if he was the only horse in the world.

Margaret and the girls stood watching from the distance as Dr. Powers strode to the side of his treasure, flushed and ebullient as she had never seen him before, as if he would embrace and kiss his great animal. But then restraining himself, he reached up and shook the hand of Francis, a young common man, a blacksmith, a fellow unaccustomed to praise and adulation, although enjoying the rarity of it amidst all the pandemonium. Margaret watched transfixed, far away, as this intersection of the pathways of two people in her life was marked, was observed, and as a great bow of gold ribbons was presented to Dr. Powers and then tied onto the bridle worn by King Arthur, regal, standing and surveying the tumult around him.

The dust was settling, the crowd drifting away. Margaret thought once again of gowns to be buttoned, dishes to be set out, tea to be brewed and poured. The trio linked arms and turned toward the lane, walking back amidst the crowd to return to their customary duties.

Later in the evening, after the grand dinner had been served and the dishes and glassware washed and polished and stored away, once again all of those in service gathered around the great plank table outside the kitchen, to eat and laugh and talk, and the fiddle was played and songs were sung. Margaret sat by the wall, knowing this might never happen again. On the far side of the room, Francis, the celebrity of the moment, was surrounded by those wanting to shake his hand, to share a drink with him.

Seeing Margaret, he broke away and crossed the room to her. "You brought me luck, Maggie, with your green scarf, and so this is for you," he said grinning down at her. He pulled from his pocket a length of striped ribbon, green and gold and blue and ivory, a resplendent trifle. She blushed, speechless at his attention. "And your scarf: I must keep it, to see me safely to America, when I go there. Which must be soon, because in America every day will be like today." And he handed her the ribbon, and clasped her hand just for a moment, and turned away.

The Proper Match

Returning to Winston Court, after three days of festivities, Margaret felt that she had become another person, someone of significance. She took up her accustomed routine, but her thoughts were elsewhere. Now it was herself, not Annie, daydreaming at breakfast.

"Are you ill, dear?" asked Jane Ellen, breaking into her reverie. Margaret started, and smiled self-consciously.

"It was such an adventure: crowds of people, and music, and horses. I have never done anything like it before." She took her dishes to the sink, washed them, and then polished them dry with a linen towel.

Dr. Powers and Elizabeth were outside in the pantry. Elizabeth was sorting an armload of flowers into piles for different vases, and she began to clip them to the proper length for their assigned container. The conversation was once again about horses, with Dr. Powers doing most of the talking.

"... A strong farmer, and a man who knows his horses. Not too many miles away, north and east of here, beyond Cashel. Two good mares he thinks he has for me, good matches for King Arthur. I will hear from him before long, I think."

This was a long speech for George Powers, and Margaret overheard it as she returned the cups and dishes to the pantry shelves. Once again in her heart she heard melodies, a rich baritone voice, a spritely fiddle. The two faces came to mind, Patrick and Francis, each of them handsome in their own way.

To America, Francis had said. She remembered things that her father had said about America, and they were bitter and bleak. This did not seem to be the same place that Francis was dreaming of – a place with rich rewards, where every day was full of excitement. For herself, all she thought she wanted was a home that was her own, where she could do things in the order she desired, rather than waiting for the command of others. She thought to herself resolutely: somehow I will reach that goal.

Her own mother came then into her mind – in a home, a farmhouse, to be sure; but not her own, and having to defer to the moods and the scoldings and even the ravings of another, someone on whom she was dependent for the roof over her head. Margaret took up a broom, and began sweeping vigorously, each stroke, each cloud of dust, underscoring her new resolve. She would find a way to be the mistress of her own home, wherever and whenever it might come to pass.

Two weeks passed, in the warmth of the summer, and the talk of horses had diminished, and then one afternoon there at the kitchen door was Patrick Fogarty, the dust of the road on his face but a smile as well. "And perhaps I could ask for a cup of tea, Miss Margaret? William said I might find you here."

She stood still like a stone for a moment or two: so the adventure had not all been in her imagination.

"Mr. Fogarty. Of course, I will heat the kettle, come right in."

Jane Ellen was scrubbing potatoes, setting the clean ones along side the two fresh cabbages already resting on the cutting board. "Ah, the man with the horses we have heard so much about. Have you spoken yet with Dr. Powers?"

"Only briefly, mum. As we were about to go up to the field to look at his great stallion, a call came for him to go deal with someone who had fallen ill, and he left in haste. He offered me a place to stay overnight, so we could continue our business in the morning. I hope not to inconvenience you."

Jane Ellen waved her hand dismissively. "You're more than welcome, to be sure. Sit and have some tea, and then perhaps the girls, Annie and Margaret, can show you the fields where the horses are grazing. 'Tis a lovely afternoon, and the view up the lane is pleasant. Have you been this way before?"

"Not for many years, since I myself was much younger. Another gentleman owned this place then, quite a horseman, and I once came to drive a pair of horses north for him, to be shown and sold at a fair in those parts. I do not recall his name."

"Ah yes, that was a splendid time for horses, though some other things fell into disarray. Lord Hubert Winston, may God rest his soul, was the builder of this house. I worked here only in his later days. He was a great man for the hunt, and for racing, but he fell into ill health and died early." Jane Ellen paused for a moment. "I am sure that William will be pleased to have you stay tonight with him, in the cottage just beyond the barns. And, of course, you will take supper here with us, after we have finished with serving the dinner upstairs."

Annie entered the kitchen, a pail in each hand, fresh from milking. "Wash your hands, Annie, and then you and Margaret can show Mr. Fogarty the way up to the horse pasture." Patrick drained his tea cup, nodded his thanks to Jane Ellen, and rose to his feet. He could have found the horse pasture on his own, to be sure, but this prospect was much more pleasant.

"So, young ladies, a fine place for horses, wouldn't you think?" said Patrick to Margaret and Annie as they left the house. He held the door open for them as they went forth into the late afternoon sun, still warm as the shadows lengthened. He had forgotten about walking with a woman, in the time since his wife's death; how his pace would slow, become more leisurely, to match his movement. And now with the two of them on his right side, Annie doing most of the talking, he could enjoy the unexpected entertainment. As usual Annie talked mainly about William, and her life ahead as his wife, and how she loved him and planned to set his life in order once they were officially wed and setting up housekeeping. Margaret was smiling, never contradicting her, occasionally catching Patrick's eye as he listened with amusement.

And he had forgotten about the lightness than came into his mood when he was with a woman, how easy it was to smile and to forget the burdens and the worries of the day, how easy it would be to remember a melody and sing a song. He thought of the evening at Blithegate, when he sang and a young woman with brown hair blushed and gazed up at him.

They reached the wooden fence around the horse pasture. King

Arthur stood some distance away, statuesque, silhouetted by the setting sun; but Sir Harry moved immediately in their direction, sending his glance toward Margaret and Annie, to see which one of them would reward him for his attention. Margaret reached deep into her pocket for the lump of sugar, and held it out to him. He accepted it, nodding gravely in thanks, and then nuzzled her shoulder before turning away and moving out into the field.

And the three of them turned as well, Margaret in the lead, walking back down the grassy path toward the house and the kitchen. William waited at the door as they approached.

"So, Patrick, my friend, let me show you where you will stay tonight, while Annie and Margaret are lending a hand in the kitchen," William said. "We have a bit of time before supper."

First to the barn, where all of the paraphernalia of operating a farm was stored, not in a muddle, but not in a particularly organized fashion either. Rakes and harnesses, bags of seeds and buckets and plows, spades and ladders. The barn was where William was truly at home, his own domain, where no one but himself knew the key to its system. The two men lingered there, not really for conversation but just for companionship; and then on to the cottage, and immediately Patrick comprehended Annie's resolve to take William in hand and organize his life once they were married. As it now was, the cottage was simply an extension of the barn, with tools and equipment on every surface, and bits of hay and dried mud on the floor. The separate sleeping room had glass in its two windows, but it was hard to tell it was glass, with the streaks of soot encrusted on it. And the two pallets for sleeping were comfortable enough, but it did not seem that the linens and blankets had been washed or aired for many weeks. There will be changes, Patrick thought to himself: I am sure that William will learn quickly.

At the supper table more talk of animals: how large a pig, how many chickens, how much milk and butter from just three cows. Winston Court had an abundance of land and very few people to be fed. And horses, beautiful horses, could graze in the open fields. Laconic conversation, few words wasted, between William and Patrick, and the others almost silent over their stew and bread.

Another summer day dawned on the morrow, sun and clouds, bird song through the windows as Margaret set Lady Amelia's tray on her table. Nothing has changed. Margaret is a servant girl, but growing older. Lady Amelia is never satisfied, always suspicious, but reconciled at least to the daily routine, to Margaret's presence. After the breakfast had been eaten, as Margaret carried the tray of dishes back down the stairs, there was Patrick once again, looking at her as she reached the kitchen.

"So, Miss Margaret, I'll be on my way now. The business about the horses is taken care of, quite happily, and I will be here again a fortnight hence. And hope to see you again then, if I may." He smiled: "I still have a song to sing you, if you remember."

His eyes on her, she felt herself a woman, not a servant girl; the sun's rays through the kitchen window cast his shadow sharp against the dark wood of the door, her shadow beside his, with light between them, but close enough to touch had they wished. Or better, had they dared: no question that the wish was there for both of them.

The long ride home, along dusty roads and over rolling hills, found Patrick thinking of the days ahead and the things that might come to pass. He might once again have a wife, a companion. His two younger children, now almost grown, might have a mother once again, though she might not be much older than they were; and Francis, old enough to be a man, might be off to America. And even, perhaps, there might be more small children underfoot, to make him young again.

Francis was the first person he saw, sitting there at the door of the house, the shadows of twilight creeping across the yard. "The two Spanish mares are sold, Frank," Patrick said. "So part of the price will be a bit more money toward your voyage. It's the time to go, for sure; there's no life here for you, no real possibility to be a man in your own right. America will be a different story." Father and son, some things they shared and some divided them.

They sat in silence for several minutes. Then Francis said, "Handbills in town say that ships leave from Cobh once or twice a month, some for Halifax, some for Boston." He paused again, not sure he could believe that this indeed might happen. "When Tom Delaney went, it was to Boston, I believe: perhaps I could find him there." He stood, moving restlessly in the yard as the idea of leaving began to possess his imagination. "And when I have made enough money I'll send it to you for the others to come join me."

Patrick's thoughts had only been of Francis leaving, not all the family, one after another. "All in good time, boy. It is not a simple matter, moving to a strange land and all that. Who knows, you may come home again some day." He took his pipe from his pocket, lit it and sat for several minutes more, as if alone. Loneliness had been the mark of his days, even with three sons in the house. The time had come to leave the solitary life behind. He emptied his pipe, returned it to his pocket, and went inside.

Gifts of Passage

Patrick Fogarty's reappearance, bringing with him as he did the two mares, gave George Powers cause for celebration. He had thought about little else since the race at Blithegate. Even after Patrick's earlier visit to Winston Court, Dr. Powers hardly dared to hope that everything would work out as perfectly as promised. That Elizabeth was so happy here in the country, that even Lady Amelia seemed satisfied with her routine, freed him to enjoy his new preoccupation with horses. He still found it difficult to think of himself as a country gentleman, but becoming engrossed in riding, and even breeding, horses was more enjoyable that he could have dreamed.

He thought of Patrick only as the man with the horses. It had not entered his mind that anything could be drawing him here to Donaldstown other than the sale of the animals. When Patrick assured him that he would come again within a month, to see if anything further must be dealt with, George Powers said it would hardly be necessary. But he was pleased with the man's concern, and said he would be happy to have him visit once again. George Powers did not know about the singing of songs outside the kitchen door in the fading light of evening, nor was he aware that another romance, another betrothal beside that of William and Annie, had crossed his threshold. And so it was a complete surprise when, at the time of Patrick's third visit, Margaret asked to speak with him and his wife and announced that she would be leaving at the month's end, to move north far into Tipperary near Roscrea, to marry and become the wife of Patrick Fogarty, widower, a man twice her age.

In the pantry, once again with an armload of flowers, Elizabeth murmured to her husband, who was clearly distressed and frustrated by the news. "There will be other girls, George, and they can be trained as well."

"Of course, of course," he said. "But she is very bright, very promising. I had hoped to see her as a competent midwife. Her touch, particularly with children, is very tender and reassuring."

"And it will be so with her own children, perhaps. We do not own her life, you know." Elizabeth's quakerly upbringing had left her uncomfortable with having servants, although she was now resigned to it. George Powers, and his mother Lady Amelia, could not imagine managing a house without those who would do the work.

Dr. Powers resolved to spend the afternoon in his study, with his books, always a source of solace. Three new volumes had just arrived, translations of Greek and Roman poetry, and he hefted them in his hands, stroking the leather bindings. The pages were still uncut, and he took out his pocket-knife to do the task, careful not to tear the paper unevenly. A solitary time, sitting at his desk, was something that gave him great consolation. The books absorbed him, and he savored the lines of poetry, almost forgotten from his school days. Thinking about ancient times was a protection and a defense, a diversion from the fearsome task of telling his mother of Margaret's imminent departure.

At the end of the afternoon, reluctantly, he rose and left his study and went to his mother's sitting room. She looked up in surprise when he knocked. After greeting her, he said abruptly, "I have some bad news. Margaret will be leaving shortly."

She looked at him sharply. "She has taken something, hasn't she?" She looked around at her treasures, to see if she could identify anything that was missing.

George Powers sighed. "Nothing of the sort, Mother. The young woman has decided to marry, and will be moving some distance from here. It is a loss for us, to be sure. She has been a great help to me, and I think she has also served you well." He paused for a moment. "I am certain that her life will be very different as a farmer's wife. I am thinking of giving her a box of books to take with her, so that she may continue to cultivate her mind. I hope that we will not completely lose contact with her: Elizabeth and I have become fond of her, as I am sure you have as well."

Lady Amelia did not respond immediately. Then she said, "She is just a servant girl, but I have seen great improvement in the time she has been here." She added, petulantly, "It is so trying, to have to train them, one after another, with little recognition of the effort it takes." After a moment, she went on, "Perhaps she will not be happy and will return to us again. And if so, of course, we will have to take her in, though she little appreciates what we do for her." She pursed her lips, clasping her hands tightly together.

The room around her, with the accumulation of vases and boxes and bowls, was now virtually her whole universe. London had faded in her memory; even Duncan was just a shadow. No one populated her days except these three – Margaret, and Elizabeth, and George – and now one of the three was to vanish as well. True, she counted people less as companionship than as irritants; but without the irritation, little feeling of any sort would be left to her.

On the following day, with the morning tea, Margaret delivered her news to Lady Amelia. The old woman glared up at her from her seat at the table. "You cannot leave without my consent, young lady, and I do not intend to permit it." Her fury was unaccustomed, but it boiled up inside her and she could not contain it.

Margaret was taken aback by the words of anger, but in Lady Amelia's eyes she saw fear, almost panic, the kind of expression that might be frozen on the face of a drowning woman as a great wave approached. But she could not reach out to her without letting go of her own hope for survival. "I shall not be leaving for some weeks yet, mum," she said soothingly.

But Lady Amelia turned away from her, took up her teaspoon, and tapped it with irritation on the napkin beside her cup. No more words came forth from her, but inside, the stew of emotions continued to simmer. Margaret curtseyed and left the room, taking a deep breath as she started down the stairs.

Elizabeth was the one who accepted the inevitability and the correctness of the development. Margaret had been quite satisfactory and, as George said, she had great promise, but that did not mean that they could claim her for the rest of her life. When she herself was young, when George Powers had first appeared, her world was suddenly transformed, and something of this sort was now happening for Margaret. No, not a young doctor from London; but still, romance in the guise of a stranger.

"I had my suspicions," Jane Ellen said when Margaret announced the news over soup at the kitchen table. "Patrick Fogarty is a responsible gentleman and all that, but these frequent visits have made him seem a bit over-solicitous about the horses which are no longer his. But he is a fine man, Margaret, and you will be well provided for. And what we will do without you I'm sure I do not know." She pulled up the corner of her apron and wiped her eyes.

Margaret felt a stinging in her own eyes. She was not accustomed to tears. Annie and Jane Ellen were her partners in affection, in the day-to-day experience of her life in the months and years spent at Winston Court. She took up a dish towel, needing to do something to distract herself, and began looking for something that needed attention, polishing, putting away in its proper place.

At the Fogarty farm, a different cast of characters was learning about momentous changes about to take place. Francis, Timothy, and Robert, all of them still living at home but working one place or another in the town, had grown accustomed to a house with no woman in it, a house where things would stay where they put them down until they had need of them once again. Ten years had passed since their mother Honoria's death, and the two younger boys had hardly any memory of her. And then the others in the family, Patrick's and Honoria's sisters and their respective husbands and children, living in smaller cottages within a quarter mile of his more substantial farm house, all of them had in mind that sooner or later the farm house would become rightfully theirs when Patrick and his boys no longer had need of the comfortable space which it provided. The rumor that Francis would soon be leaving for America had brightened the glimmer of hope that each of them held dear.

And now, for each of them, the news of an alien newcomer about to arrive planted the seeds of resentment, the assurance that this Margaret would be a loathsome tyrant. Only Francis had another reason, another target for his resentment, and he could not bring himself to speak to his own father, or to anyone else, of the deep wound which his father's marrying would inflict into his own heart.

And so he packed his bag, and gave his notice to James Murray the blacksmith, and sent letters by post to various and sundry acquaintances from Tipperary who had left before, who were thought to be successfully settled in Boston, giving the word that he hoped soon to be joining them in that city, and would be looking for a position and a place to stay once he arrived. And then, a week before Patrick planned his next trip to Winston Court to bring Margaret home as his bride, Francis said his abrupt farewells and left, heading south to Cork and then to Cobh to take passage on a ship bound west across the ocean, toward the unknown but certainly more welcoming possibilities than the ones he faced at home.

Patrick's dim awareness that he was in his eldest son's disfavor was completely overshadowed by his anticipation of the new bright chapter in his own life. He gave Francis money – more than he intended, almost the full price of his passage – and he gave him his blessing, and a pair of boots sturdy enough to see him through the winters in America, which he knew to be harsher than those in Ireland. There were no tears at the moment of farewell, but it was, he thought, an amiable parting.

"And the day will come when you will return, or when the other boys will leave here to join you," Patrick said, with his hand still resting on his son's shoulder.

"That may be, pa; time will tell." Francis pulled free and turned away. He picked up his belongings and walked toward the road.

Patrick walked back into the house, seeing anew the windows without curtains, the bare shelves with only enough cups and plates for the five of them to use, the half-dozen pegs in the wall the only storage for clothing not being worn on their backs at the moment. It was a good house, solid and well-proportioned, and with a woman's hand it would become a real home again.

Margaret, walking the hallways of Winston Court, tried to imagine this next unknown abode: not the snug small dwelling of her childhood, not the cottage beside the barn where Annie would soon be living, not the resplendent expanse of Blithegate or Winston Court. And whatever the house might be, what would she have within it? Nothing of her own, except for a few changes of clothes and a nightgown and a shawl. Patrick would provide for her, Jane Ellen had said. But, she thought, there are ways I must provide for myself. Not with the enormous painted portraits hanging in the great hall, or with Lady Amelia's vases and bowls. But pots and pans, at least, and a rolling-pin, and a good ladle. The things she would need, that she did not have, began to fill every corner of her mind. She had come here without possessions, and she was also leaving empty-handed.

In three days Patrick would be coming once again, and she would pay her farewells and leave with him for a different life. After she had brought the breakfast tray down from Lady Amelia's room, she washed dishes and put them away once again, almost if not quite the last time. The pantry shelves held dishes and glassware and silver far in excess of what would ever be used by this small family, lined up meticulously and regularly polished and dusted. She placed each piece carefully in its proper compartment, the silver tableware in its assigned sections in the drawers beneath the countertop.

And then up to the study, with its rows and rows of books, more than she had dreamed existed when she first came to Winston Court. Now they had become her familiars, with whom she could sit in silent discourse when she was alone in the room. After today, tomorrow, the next day, perhaps she would never again share in this conversation.

On the morning before the final day, Lady Amelia greeted her arrival with her customary glare of irritation, and then said something out of the ordinary.

"Sit down, girl. There are some things I must tell you." Margaret obeyed, seating herself on the bench by the window, facing the old woman at her table. "First, you must keep your own counsel, and not rely on anyone, even this man who is to be your husband, to always have your best interest in mind. Men are easily distracted," she took a deep breath, "And the things they are occupied with may have little to do with your well-being."

Margaret was transfixed by Lady Amelia's little speech; it seemed to have just begun.

"Second, you must cultivate a resilience within yourself which will stay intact even when you find yourself in harsh and challenging circumstances. Life sometimes carries you to places where you never expected to be, and where you doubt you can survive. But survive you will.

"And lastly, keep some small thing safe to remind you of these instructions I have given you. And so I give you this." She unpinned the ivory brooch, always on her gown or shawl, and pressed it into Margaret's hand. "Now get back to the kitchen, girl. I am sure there is work for you to do there."

Once again, Margaret felt tears stinging her eyes. She would have liked to embrace Lady Amelia; but she bowed her head and curtseyed, and went out the door of the room.

When she reached the kitchen, Lady Elizabeth and Dr. Powers were waiting at the door of the pantry, each with a parcel beside them on the counter.

"We have a few things for you to include in your packing, Margaret." Lady Elizabeth pulled forth the first bundle. "When I came here to Winston Court, I found an abundance of good linens already here, and so I would like you to have these few towels and sheets from the ones I brought from Dublin." The parcel was wrapped in heavy paper and firmly tied.

George Powers cleared his throat. "And I also have something to give you: just a few books, but these should be a reminder of the things you have learned here, so that you will continue to cultivate your mind and put it to good use." He moved the small wooden box, and opened its lid to show the dozen or so books within it.

Margaret could not tear her eyes away from the books in the box. That she would be the owner of books – not just one volume, but a whole box of them – amazed her. It was more startling than becoming mistress of her own house. She lifted one up in her hands, and then there was another, and another. This gift – both of the gifts – erased for a moment her servanthood. But she could not embrace them; only curtsey, once again. "Thank you for all you have given me," she started. She could not say 'this has been my home,' which was not quite true; but then she said, "Your care for me has helped me become what I am." The two nodded to her, pleased, touched as well.

In the kitchen, when Jane Ellen put the supper on the table, she waited until Annie and William and Margaret were seated, and then left the room for a moment. When she returned, in her hands was a creamy white bundle. She shook it loose, and held it high for them to see, and then draped it around Margaret's shoulders: a knitted shawl, soft as a cloud, with an intricate pattern covering it. "You are very fortunate, young lady, that this is finished, with only these few weeks before your departure, and having to make it when you were out of sight." Jane Ellen smiled her delight at the look of shock on Margaret's face. Something to be worn just for the beauty of it was a rare experience. With my green dress, and the ivory brooch, she thought, there is nothing more I could want.

ROSCREA, COUNTY TIPPERARY

1821

Homemaking

The house, Patrick Fogarty's farm house, was set back from the road by a dozen and a half yards, and the rutted lane led in through the stone wall and on to the shed, which had an open covered area for the horses and an enclosure for the hay mow. It was several months now since Margaret had first arrived, riding in on the wagon beside the man who had become her husband, casting a critical eye on the yard that was just an overgrown meadow, with barely discernable traces of the garden it once had been. And would be again, she resolved: the memory of Lady Elizabeth's rose bushes and lilies and daisies was then fresh in her mind.

But now, as the days grew shorter and the west wind had more of a chill in it, she had little time to spend in the garden. Winter would have to do my weeding, she thought, and in springtime she would bring things into good order.

In the meantime, she was faced with the matter of making the farm house into a home. The house gave her nothing to complain about, but much to be done. And no stairs to climb or descend between the tasks, praise the Lord, she thought to herself. Of course, there was the ladder that led to the loft; but the loft was nothing she had to trouble herself about. The boys slept there, and aside from reminding them to bring down their bedclothes and shirts and trousers for washing on laundry day, the loft was no concern of hers. They had a need for a space which she would not enter, and that was fine by her, thank you.

The house itself with its three rooms, its stove for cooking and heating the main room and bringing the teakettle to a boil: this was now her domain, and she devoted all her energy to bringing every inch of it under her control. First with the broom, sweeping and sweeping and then sweeping again, to drive out every cobweb and bit of dust and muddy boot track that had accumulated in the years since the death of Honoria. And then, after the broom, the bucket of hot soapy water, first scrubbing the windows and then the stone door step, and the hearth, and every bit of the woodwork, and the few bare shelves where the tableware and the cooking pots had been sitting, leaving behind their outline in the dust.

During the first few days, Patrick had chided her for her overflowing energy. "No need to exert yourself so, Margaret," he protested. He did not want her to think that she was just a servant here, just a cleaning woman. But she paid him no attention, and he came to see that she was taking possession, claiming it as her own. And as it became hers, it became his once again, no longer haunted by Honoria's ghost.

Curtains had never hung at the windows. But now, as the weather grew cold, Margaret went into the town of Roscrea and searched through the shops until she found some woolen piece goods, checked in blue and white, soft and warm enough to keep out the drafts, beautiful enough to hang in the sitting room of a palace rather than just a farm house. She paid for it with the coins she had saved from her housekeeping money, and took it home and cut and stitched it and hung it from rods in each of the windows before Patrick had any inkling of what she was about. And then she found some blue and white striped linen, long enough to cover the table, and she bought that piece and hemmed it and spread it the length of the table-top, and in the center she placed two candle-sticks, and it looked as if it could be in the finest house in town.

At least once a week each of the sisters would come by – Honoria's older sister Irene, and Patrick's sister Deirdre, two years younger than he was. They did not come together, but it seemed they conspired to draw up a long list of Margaret's flaws and inadequacies.

Irene came first, three days after Margaret had arrived with Patrick and they had gone and exchanged their vows before the priest. The few things Margaret had brought with her were unpacked and stored away, the box of books placed on a low shelf beside a chair.

Irene did not knock, but pushed open the door and entered. "Are my nephews here?" she asked, with no introductions or pleasantries. The boys were her thread of connection with her sister, whom she still could not think of as dead and gone.

"You must be Irene. The kettle is hot; have you time for a cup of tea?" Margaret felt herself to be the unwelcome intruder before the woman at the doorway. "The boys are all working, I fear, and Francis is gone, left for America two days before I arrived here. And will be missed by everyone, to be sure." Her smile was not returned; Irene Maloney was looking for someone she would never see again.

The woman in the dark threadbare dress avoided her eyes. "When the boys come back, I need their help with the hay. It is more than I can do to get it in before the rain." And Irene was out the door and gone, without a single pleasant word out of her mouth.

Margaret looked out the doorway at the receding figure. "Come again, Irene Maloney, when you have more time to spend." That some did not want her there was no question; but she was here, and this was her home. Patrick knew little of the ways of women; he thought this strangeness would pass. There was no need for unsociability among neighbors. The day might come when you might need a helping hand.

Deirdre Fogarty was little better when it came to friendliness. No one was good enough for her brother Patrick: Honoria had not been, and this Margaret person seemed to be cut of the same cloth. And she had brought not even a daughter or son into the household so far, to carry on the Fogarty blood and make things right.

Margaret had been sitting in a chair at the table, one of the books open before her, when she sensed someone at the door. She turned, and rose to greet Deirdre, but the woman was on her way without speaking a word. That was the first time, and after that, almost every day, as Margaret hung laundry out to dry or crossed the yard to gather eggs, she could see Deirdre watching from afar, from the front of her own cottage or peering out a window. It was as if she was regarded as a different species.

"She shouldn't bother you," Patrick said, seeing Margaret staring toward the neighboring cottage. "She's always like that, hostile, critical beyond reason. She's a good woman, just very protective of her own."

"It seems I am not to be one of her own," Margaret said softly. "I want to belong here, Patrick."

"This is your house, not theirs. More sugar in her tea will not make Deirdre into a sweet and pleasant person. Perhaps the day will come when she will be different, but for now, this is something just to be endured. This place is ours, not Irene's, not Deirdre's, whatever they may think or say." Patrick was not given to long speeches; but now that he had a wife of his own once again, he was determined that the place where he lived not be a pot constantly boiling over with tension and unpleasantness. He put his arms around Margaret. "Push them out of your mind, my dear. There is too much in life to be enjoyed to let them ruin it."

She felt the stiffness leave her back and shoulders, and laid her head against his chest. He was no longer a stranger to her. In the time since she had come north with him, he had become her protector. In the days at Winston Court she had learned to fend for herself, to value the support of Dr. Powers and his wife and even the directives of Lady Amelia, but they were not her own people, nor was she theirs. Now, with Patrick, she knew that she belonged to him, and he to her.

Although in truth his mind was often more preoccupied with the horses than with herself. On a day when there was to be a fair, in Roscrea or in any other town within a reasonable distance, she could be certain that he would be up and gone before the dawn, wanting to be the first one to set his eye on any beasts that would be up for sale. It was rare that he actually bought an animal. His fields could pasture six or eight horses, not more than that, and he sought out fine specimens, usually young ones, which he could feed and groom and train and then sell for a handsome profit. The word was out that Patrick Fogarty was the man to see when you were looking for a promising horse.

The Fogarty farm was a good piece of land, one that had been cultivated by his father and his grandfather and earlier generations of the family. It was due to something of a miracle, as well as a bit of deviousness, that the land had not been lost in the time of great injustice in years past. Patrick had learned well from those before him that one must toe a careful line to avoid such conflict and unpleasantness. Some said that this made him less than a man of principle: that he would rather avoid an argument than put his life and land on the line for something he believed. He saw it as simple common sense, that belligerence accomplished less than civil negotiation. Sometimes an agreement was reached that left one side or the other with a bit of a sense of bitterness, that the balance struck was not exactly even; but even so, a settlement had been reached.

All of this had nothing to do with Margaret. She was not a woman who sought compromises. She liked to find some clarity about an issue, and then throw her whole heart and all her energy into it. If she was not in agreement with something that was happening, she would rather keep her own counsel.

The boys, Patrick's two sons still at home, had adjusted to her presence. It was more as if she were an older sister, someone they could tease a bit, than a substitute mother to whom they owed obedience. Whatever resentment they might have felt soon vanished, as they became accustomed to the aroma of food on the stove. None of them were lovers of books and reading: that was Margaret's affair, and they left the pile beside her chair for her.

The walk to town, whatever the weather, provided Margaret with a time of her own, an escape from Deirdre and Irene's watchful eyes. She returned by mid-day, in time to stir the fire and heat a pot of stew. One day as she returned, Deirdre was standing at the door, and for the first time spoke directly to her. "A man was here asking for you: a gentleman, on a big black horse. Margaret Hickey, he asked for. Margaret Fogarty, you mean, I said. And what would he be wanting?" Her tone was unpleasant, suspicious even.

Margaret entered the house and put her parcels down on the table. "Did he give you his name? I know no one who would come looking for me here."

Deirdre turned and left the doorway, saying nothing more. When the man came again she would be watching.

Three days later, as the afternoon waned, Margaret heard a knock at the door. The rain had subsided, but there was still a fine mist in the air, and a chill breeze stirring to carry the moisture away. She opened the door to find a man of medium height and graying hair, not similar in appearance but with the same mannerisms and cultured way of speaking as Dr. George Powers.

"Would you be Margaret Hickey?" he asked somewhat hesitantly. "I am Charles Kingsbury, Dr. Charles Kingsbury. My good friend George Powers told me of you, that you had moved here to marry, and that he was sorely disappointed to lose you." He removed his spectacles, wet from the mist and rain, and rubbed them dry with his handkerchief. "I have a dispensary in town, where I see many people from the countryside, and their children as well. More than I can deal with, as a matter of fact. Dr. Powers encouraged me to search you out, and perhaps to employ you as an assistant. The children are a particular problem: such simple things would make them much healthier." He sighed, and put his spectacles on once again.

Margaret stood silent. This was, of course, the man of whom Deirdre was so suspicious.

Charles Kingsbury spoke once again. "The dispensary I could manage by myself, but now there is the fever hospital as well, not yet fully constructed, but before many months pass it will also need my attention."

She then spoke slowly, not sure quite how to respond. "My husband Patrick is not here, and I must talk with him before I could give you any answer." She paused, thinking back to the days spent with Dr. Powers, the crying children, the worried mothers, the adventure of learning about diseases and treatments and cures. She had resigned herself to all that being in the past.

First she must explain to Patrick, tell him about the work that she had done with Dr. Powers, that she had learned skills she did not want to forget. Soap and water, George Powers had instructed her, are as important and powerful as any medication. And inoculation against the pox can be a great protection, insurance that a child will be more likely to grow to adulthood, not carried off suddenly by a terrible fever. All of these lessons, spread by the good physicians, were making Ireland into a more populous country, where children ate potatoes and cabbage and milk and eggs, and played in the farmyards and worked in the fields, and more and more often lived a long life. And then, as adults, they found that they had no land, no home, and packed a trunk and went away, off across the westward ocean to America, where there was work and land, and even meat on the table.

When she sat with Patrick at the table that evening, she asked him, "Do you know Dr. Charles Kingsbury?"

"Know of him, though I have never met the man. He has been in Roscrea for many years."

"He came here today, on the advice of Dr. Powers, who he said was an old friend." She paused for a few minutes. "When I was at Winston Court, one of my duties was to accompany Dr. Powers to his dispensary in Fermoy, and assist in treating the young children. I loved doing that, and I learned many things from him." She took the teakettle from the stove, and poured the steaming water into the teapot. "Dr. Kingsbury came here today, to ask if I would be able to assist him at his dispensary in Roscrea. It would give me great pleasure, if you do not object."

Deirdre had already spoken to her brother about the strange man who had come looking for his wife. Deirdre had something to say to him almost every day, something intended to breed suspicion and ill will. He knew his sister thought she had his best interests at heart; but the world was different, more complicated, than the simple melodrama she laid forth.

It would be unusual, to say the least, for a housewife to go and work for someone, whoever that someone might be. But Margaret was unusual, of that he was sure. That was what had drawn him to her, not just the green dress, and the direct and inquiring look in her eyes, and the persuasiveness of the words that came out of her mouth.

"I have no objection, Margaret my dear. Dr. Kingsbury is, I am sure, an honorable man, and you have the common sense to dictate your arrangements with him. And we may all profit from what you learn, some day in the future."

* * *

Patrick, my brother, is my greatest treasure, however neglectful he may be of me. When I could barely walk, hardly more than a babe, he would hold both my hands and coax my steps forward, laughing with delight. That is all I need; his hands on mine, and his laughter. But for all these years now he disregards me – first for Honoria, and now this Margaret person. Without them life would be harmonious – I need nothing more than this wee cottage of my own, and I could milk his cow, and gather the eggs and feed the chickens, and I can cook the potatoes until they are tender and piping hot. He needs nothing more, and I have this to give. But the elegant Margaret is too haughty to be satisfied with potatoes and chick's eggs – gentleman caller indeed, asking for her by name, with no concern for decency at all. The day will come when she'll be gone, off to some scandalous goings-on, and Patrick will remember for sure that I am the one who cares for him, who always has, who will not run off after some gentleman on horseback.

* * *

"Ah, good: I was certain you would come." Charles Kingsbury looked up from his chair as Margaret entered the door and closed it behind her. Beside Dr. Kingsbury was a wooden bench, and a young mother sat holding her small child, who was wailing dolefully as the doctor passed his hands through the tangled hair. "Lice, of course, and none too clean either," he said to Margaret. "No way to stay healthy without soap and water: prayer alone will not keep disease away. I am sure you have heard this all before from my friend George Powers."

Margaret looked around the small dispensary. It was spotless but cluttered, so much like Dr. Powers' office in Fermoy. The doorway at the back of the room was hung with a dark curtain, from the top to the floor: beyond it, she was sure, was the examining room, with its high narrow table. Dr. Kingsbury turned from the young patient to his desk, with its piles of paper, and made quick notations on the sheet before him. He spoke again to the mother: "This soap, now: use it daily on his hair, and after each washing go through the hair with your fingers, and remove every louse, and every egg as well." He had said this to her before, with other children on her lap, but each time it was as if it was new and alien information. "The lice bring disease, and it is most important to have a healthy child." He smiled, and nodded brusquely, and turned away; the mother gathered her small son in her arms, bowed her head toward Margaret, and left the dispensary.

"So, now: tell me what you know from your time with Dr. Powers." Charles Kingsbury turned his eyes toward Margaret, motioning her to the chair before him. She took a deep breath: how could she describe it all?

"Dr. Powers goes regularly to provide care and attend patients in Fermoy. Some of his services are to the military men at the garrison, who have been injured or fallen ill, and I had little to do with that. But he also gave care to many mothers and children, just as you were doing a few moments ago, and he trained me to help him, particularly with the young children. And smallpox, too: he was sometimes able to obtain the matter for inoculating against the disease, and he instructed me so that I could do this with the children whose parents brought them to him. And he allowed me to read some of the books in his study, and this opened my eyes to many things about health and disease."

"And midwifery: what do you know of those skills?"

Her face colored as she answered. "Almost nothing, sir, except what I have read in books. I do not yet have children, and I have never been present at a birth."

"No matter: all in good time. There is a great need for midwives who understand about cleanliness, about protecting both the infant and the mother. Perhaps some day. . . ." His voice trailed off, and he sat for a moment. Then he went on. "What I would like to propose, if you are willing, is that you come to assist me twice a week, to undertake the same duties as you performed with Dr. Powers. I will pay you decently, of course, and you may be able to save something toward the day when you have your own children to care for. Would that be satisfactory?"

"I would be so happy to do so. I have missed it very much, since I left Winston Court. Yes, yes, I would love to work for you." She could not stop smiling.

Fevers

The two children, James and Maureen, filled the house with their voices. James was the older of the two, and he was happiest when he could trail after Patrick's elder sons, whatever task they might be doing about the house or the farmyard. He tried manfully to make his stride as long as their own, though he was little more than half their height. And Maureen was a ray of sunlight, happy whatever she was doing, and happiest when she was with her Aunt Deirdre, who was morose and glum and hostile but unable to resist the little girl's charms. So day by day, week by week, she became a bit less unpleasant. Deirdre was still unforgiving about Margaret's presence. But she seemed able to ignore the incontrovertible truth that it was Margaret who mothered Maureen, Patrick who fathered her, and that they therefore had a hand in brightening her days.

Patrick had been absent now for almost three months. Something extraordinary had happened early in the summer: the field of beautiful young mares, a half dozen of them, had all been sold, for a price so good that he could not resist it. And Patrick without a horse to groom and train and caress was a lost man, however much money he might have put away from the sale. And so he paced back and forth, and went to the fairs, looking for a promising young horse that might be a suitable replacement, and became more restive each time he returned not leading an animal behind him. And then his mood changed, not to one of happiness, but a different determination.

"It's wiser to wait until spring, Margaret," he said one night. "And I have another opportunity: not for a long time, but just until December. The new railroad, you know, is under construction from Dublin south to Cork. It is not something I could do forever, but the money is good, and Matt Scanlon has written me and promised a foreman's job. And the money, Margaret, will buy a team of fine horses, something to fill the field once again."

Patrick was not a man who could be persuaded to do something against his will. She would miss him; the children would miss him. But they were happy and settled here, and she had reached some accommodation with Deirdre and even with Irene. On the days when she went to work at Dr. Kingsbury's dispensary, the two small children stayed under Deirdre's watchful eye, and when she returned it was with an extra bit of cheese, or a box of tea, or a jar of jam for Deirdre and for Irene as well.

The hospital was claiming more and more of Charles Kingsbury's time – not that the fearful cholera, already making its presence felt in the large cities, had appeared in Roscrea; but there were always people too sick and too poor to be cared for at home. No one should die alone, Dr. Kingsbury was in the habit of saying – alone by the side of the road, or in some hovel where no one else lived any more. Sometimes the hospital could offer some healing, but at least it could provide the solace of companionship in the final hours.

Margaret spent no time at the hospital, which was outside of the town and set against a hillside with open fields around it. Death was not something she chose to think about. When mothers came to her at the dispensary with squalling infants, or young farmhands with a festering wound that needed to be cleaned and treated and bandaged, she thought only about life, and did her work energetically, and believed that all would be well. And when Dr. Kingsbury was able to obtain some of the matter for smallpox inoculation, and posted an announcement of the day and time when people could receive it, she knew there would be a line waiting for her, one arm after another extended for her to swab it clean and scratch the skin and rub the powdered dried scabrous stuff into it, and then wrap it carefully with a clean cotton bandage, sure in the knowledge that few would become ill and many would stay healthy.

When she was still at Winston Court her labors for Dr. Powers had been simply that of a household servant, intelligent and skilled in doing the tasks he directed when she accompanied him to Fermoy. But now, at Charles Kingsbury's dispensary, she was somehow more independent, doing things she knew how to do herself, not just things she was told to do. And she had become a familiar face to people on the street as well, not just a housewife going to market, but a person in her own right.

During the months while Patrick was away, she missed him, his warmth and friendliness and the songs he sang in the evening; and the children missed him as well, the two young ones who always ran to greet him when they heard his voice outside the door. But even with him gone, there was a comfort and tranquility in the house, a sense that everything was in order, and that he would soon come again and they would all be together. He would be home, he had promised, in time for Christmas. They all had that to look forward to.

She was not ready to see him once again entering at the door when he came, as the late afternoon winter darkness fell one day in the first week of December. Maureen ran to him first, jumped into his arms, wordless with delight. She threw her arms around his neck like a vise, and Patrick could only smile at Margaret, his eyes tired but aglow.

"Earlier than I expected, my dear. The work was going well, but too many sickened with the terrible fever that started in Dublin. So things are suspended until the disease subsides. And I came right home, of course: where else would I go?"

He lowered Maureen to the floor, and moved into the room to embrace Margaret. James entered the room, wanting to be picked up and held tight, but shrinking from appearing too sentimental – a girl could be forgiven, but not a growing lad. It was minutes before Patrick was conscious that his young son was there, and then he turned with a great cry and swept the boy up in a bear hug, as James squealed with delight. Together again, a perfect and cherished moment.

The thick ragged blanket that had hung around Patrick's shoulders as he entered fell to the floor in a pile, and he kicked it aside into the corner of the room.

"The men have all gone their separate ways, those who are still alive. Matt Scanlon, my good friend – he is gone, and many others too. He gave me this blanket when he sickened, telling me to keep warm, to care for myself and remember him. So suddenly it happened, like a bad dream, but far too real for a dream."

He sat down in the chair, James still in his arms, and now Maureen climbing on him too.

"You need something to eat. We all are hungry: you sit with the children, while I stir up the fire and put the kettle on." Margaret came to her senses, put potatoes and water in a pot, washed out the old leaves from the teapot and spooned in fresh ones. She called back the memories of the daily routine before he had gone away and embraced them once again, laying out plates and cups, knives and forks and spoons, on the blue and white tablecloth.

Soon the potatoes were on the table, and butter and milk and tea, and a generous slice of precious cheese. Maureen was asleep, still clinging fast to Patrick. He lifted her carefully as he changed seats, turning and placing James on the bench beside him. The food was less important than this feast for his eyes, gathered around him. Wordless, he reached across the table to take Margaret's hand. She spooned two potatoes onto his plate, and poured his cup full of steaming tea. The flicker of the candles made every movement of her hands into a dance of shadows on the walls, as if they were surrounded by crowds sharing their silent celebration.

And then to bed, the children bundled on their cots, Margaret and Patrick entwined beneath the blanket on their bed. Sleep came quickly, but Patrick stayed restless with the torment of the things he had seen, men falling ill and dying so suddenly that they could not even seek help. His throat was dry, his head hurt as he thought of the sudden pain, the spasms of vomiting, strong men suddenly dropping where they stood and unable to help themselves. Lord, deliver us, he prayed silently.

In early morning when he awoke Margaret was already dressed, making tea, laying out clothes for the children. She was in and out of the sleeping room quietly, preparing for the day, not wanting to disturb him until he was ready to rise.

Finally he sat up. "So early, Margaret: where are you off to?"

"Good day, Patrick. Not yet, of course, but I must spend some time, an hour or two at least, at the dispensary. No sooner did the fever hospital open than it was almost full, and Dr. Kingsbury spends much of his time there. So other things, the simple complaints, are left for me to deal with." She sat beside him and smiled. "I will not be too long, and Deirdre will watch over Maureen. If James is a bother to you, he can help the boys: there are still potatoes to be dug, even at this late date, and they have been delaying the task as long as possible."

He held her hands in his, tightly, drawing strength from being together with her once again. Probably it had been a mistake to go away, however welcome the new money in his pockets might be. Tiredness still overwhelmed him. It was so good to be home.

After a few moments, Margaret pulled herself free, and rose, and put on her cloak. "The older boys will be awake and wanting to be with you before long. Each has his stories to tell you, and wants to know about the great railroad, and when they will see it for themselves." She caught his hand once more, and then went out and closed the door.

* * *

It is quite predictable, who will sicken and die: I have always believed this to be so, and in all my years of practice, nothing could shake me from this belief. True, building this hospital has been one of my great goals, but that is because there are so many poor souls who will not follow the most basic guidance about caring for their own health. Cleanliness, pure air, wholesome food – no matter how many times they are told, they remember nothing. And so they suffer. And in the months since the hospital has been open, the same thing has been true. The invalids coming through the door, whether walking under their own power or carried, insensate as if they had too much strong drink (and sometimes indeed they had), were as much in need of nourishment and a warm bath as anything I could do for them.

But now, something new, very troubling. This new awful malady, just as I have heard from Dublin and abroad, is quite indiscriminate in who it strikes. When

Patrick Fogarty, Margaret's husband, appeared at the door,
I assumed that he brought a message for me from her. But
no – he was gripped with the violent fever, and the spasms
and the purging, just as I have heard; and by the end of
the afternoon, gasping, he was gone, dead, just like the sev-
eral others who have appeared out of nowhere in the last
two weeks. And all that could be done was to wrap him
in a sheet and lay him down like the others in the great
pit that has been dug out behind, and covered with quick-
lime, to discourage contagion. And now with heavy heart
I must walk out of here, and go and tell Margaret Hickey,
Margaret Fogarty, the dreadful news.

* * *

The door was ajar when Charles Kingsbury reached the cottage. Inside he could see Margaret sitting, the girl in her lap with a tattered blanket wrapped around her. This was a different Margaret than the one he knew – not confident and self-possessed, but with a look of wild desperation about her.

"Dr. Kingsbury! I never thought to see you here. I returned, and could not find Patrick anywhere; and my child Maureen is so ill, so suddenly. She cries in pain, and gasps; she cannot take food or water, or keep anything in her stomach. This came on suddenly, they say, an hour before I returned home, and now she is barely alive. Oh, where is Patrick? I need him so!" She broke off, suddenly aware that it was unusual to have the man appear at her door, and that she did not know what it could mean.

"Let me look at her more closely, Margaret." He folded back the blanket from the child's face, and saw what he feared – the darkening color brought on by the fever, the eyes glittering but not seeing. She seemed to shrink in size as he watched her. And then a terrible moan, and a gasp, and her breathing stopped.

Margaret sat rigid, knowing but not believing what was happening before her eyes. She clasped Maureen, what was left of her, tighter and tighter to her breast.

"She is gone," the doctor said gently, shaking his head.

"Patrick – I need Patrick. Where is he? Why is he not here when I need him so?"

"I came here to tell you – he also is gone, with the fever and the spasms, just like this child of yours. He came to us thinking that we could help him, and there was nothing to be done. From the time he arrived until he died was just two or three hours. All of the things we think we know, and in the face of this, nothing." He stopped: he was talking more to himself than to her. ""He is already in the earth, Margaret: that is all we know to do to stop this plague."

She stared up at him, waiting for the nightmare to pass. In a few moments, much of her life had blown away, like dead leaves from a winter tree. "What am I to do?" she said despairingly, looking down at her dead child, and up again at the man standing beside her.

"For the sake of the others, and of yourself as well, she must be buried. Come now; gather the blanket around her, and I will go with you. A terrible thing, but at least she will rest with her father." He put his arm around Margaret's shoulders, suddenly terribly weary, and led her out the door.

Dispossession

Margaret was numb as she walked back home from the hospital grounds, her arms empty, her life torn apart. All that was left for her was James, still a little boy, a boy without father or sister.

As she approached the cottage she could see Deirdre standing, blocking the doorway.

"Margaret Hickey: what kind of wife, what kind of mother are you, who cannot even keep your own family alive? Nursing everyone else's children is fine indeed, but where are we now, without Patrick, without my darling Maureen?" Deirdre's voice was shrill, strident, her look of loathing as intense as it had been when Margaret had first arrived in Roscrea.

In the dimness inside the cottage, sitting cowering on the bench at the table, was James. He bound his arms tight across his chest. The boy was frightened, uncomprehending. Something terrible had happened, and he did not understand what it had been.

Margaret forced her way past Deirdre, hung her cloak on the peg beside the door, and went to sit down beside James. Her own grief diminished as she felt his form, rigid, almost trembling, give way and soften at her touch. She drew him close.

She spoke quietly to the hard figure of Deirdre, still standing at the door.

"This is our home, Deirdre. We have all suffered a great loss. I can barely think about it. James does not know what to do with what has just happened. Please be kind, be gentle. We must put our lives back together."

"Not your home, missus. If Frank were still here, God bless him, it would be his now; but with him far away it will fall to one of the two boys, Timothy or Robert, for it is rightfully theirs. First son of first wife, that would be Robert, and if he should leave for another place, then Timothy. Not you, missus, with your strange fancy ways, who has brought only misery with you."

Margaret felt tears welling up. She had not been able to weep, in all the devastation of the last few hours. Now these words were thrown at her like knives, like cudgels, and not just at her but at the small boy James as well.

"Good night, Deirdre. We need to be alone, and to sleep." She detached herself from the boy, and lit a candle, and went and firmly closed the door.

Bread and butter and tea, nothing more. They ate in silence, and she cleared away the cups and plates, and took the boy in her lap in the great chair, the chair that had always been Patrick's seat. And when the candles guttered, she blew them out and walked with the boy into the sleeping room. He took off his shoes and trousers, and laid down on the cot, alone, small, numb. She pulled the blanket over him, and he closed his eyes, drifting to sleep.

She sat on the edge of her bed, wishing she were anywhere else than alone in the bed in this room, a room in the house that was no longer hers. So suddenly, a chapter had ended and another begun, and she had no notion what it would be about. As she lowered herself onto the bed, and pulled the coverlet around her, she heard the older boys, Timothy and Robert, enter the house and climb the ladder into the loft above, their voices low. They knew of the deaths; but what would they know, what would they think, of her and James? She could not think of herself as an outcast. She must make a plan. Her mind was full of the fragments of life and death, the anxiety of the changes at hand, the anticipation of being rejected and driven forth. Sleep would not come, only a multitude of torments. She clenched her hands, and unclenched them again, and turned onto her side. Finally, she drew the coverlet around her, and rose quietly, and went to the other room to sit in Patrick's chair. There, in the cold and dark, she finally fell asleep.

She awakened to a rapping on the door. The morning light shone through the window. James was already awake, sitting on the bench beside the table, rubbing his eyes sleepily. The rapping came again, more insistently.

The coverlet, folded, she placed over the back of the chair, and smoothed her hair with her hands. It did not matter what she looked like. A part of her life was behind her, the part spent in Roscrea.

She opened the door. On the stone step outside stood Charles Kingsbury, hat in hand, struggling to find words.

"Margaret. I know how deeply your loss. . ." His voice trailed off. "You are invaluable to me, to everyone who needs your skilled help here. I know you must take some time to pull life back together, but I wish to assure you that I shall pay you adequately to provide for your needs and those of the boy. And you should not hesitate to call on me for help, whatever you may need."

The first words anyone had spoken to her since Deirdre's outburst yesterday. She looked at him, and then bowed her head.

"It seems I will no longer have a home here. Others lay claim to it, and I have not yet thought about what I am going to do. But thank you: your help gives me some hope." She stopped for a moment. "And James – he does not understand what has happened, only that there is suddenly no welcome, no love here for either of us."

She spoke calmly, in a monotone, but Dr. Kingsbury saw a different person than the one he knew. Her face was drawn, and her straight figure seemed to have shrunken in the last two days.

"Other places can be found to live," he said, with a certain note of desperation. The dispensary and the hospital – people thought of him when they spoke about them, but these were not things that he could manage just by himself. In truth, it was Margaret's skill that provided so much of the care, and he would be hard pressed to deal with all the demands without her. "I must go back to the hospital: every day more people are appearing with the fever. But you can rely on my help. Stay with the boy today and tomorrow, and come to talk with me at the dispensary on the next morning. We will make a plan." He smiled, expressing a confidence he did not really feel. These family matters, here in Tipperary, were things he found hard to understand. Even when he had first spoken to Deirdre Fogarty, years ago, he had felt the note of hostility toward the newcomer. No attempt was made to disguise it, to give any appearance of civility. So often, he thought, people seemed to invest more in cultivating animosities than in finding a way to live peaceably together. No wonder that maladies crept in and captured them so easily.

He reached out and put his hand on her shoulder, saying nothing, and then placed his hand on the head of the boy. Words could do little. After a few moments, he nodded gravely to Margaret, and turned and left the house. A place for them to live: it sounded so easy, but there were complications on every side. She was a person of some independence, and would not willingly become a household servant once again. He thought about the great Georgian houses that dotted the countryside. Living in any of them would be entrapment for her; and few of their owners would tolerate the thought of a single woman with a child under their roof, even if she was a respectable widow.

The teakettle: a cup of tea, and some bread, she thought. "James, fetch the cups and plates," she commanded. They must begin with the most ordinary things, just as they had always done, and somehow the pieces of their lives that were missing would no longer loom so stark and frightening. James did her bidding: only two cups, two plates.

Charles Kingsbury pulled his cloak more closely around himself as he mounted his horse and headed northeast on the road into town. The chill wind, the moisture in the air, did nothing to help his mood. He took such pride in his work – the building of the hospital, the constant effort to promote health in the community. He had not time to think of anything else: no time to marry, no time to feel anything at all. As he rode along the stone walls bordering the river on the southern boundary of the town, he examined the dark rocks, glistening from the rain. They were so firm, so immovable, just like the walls of the fever hospital, containing and restraining something that could run amok, flood everything around it, destroy the order and harmony of the civilized world. What he had found so enthralling about Margaret Hickey was that she was so much like himself, cool, efficient, competent. Now that he had seen something else of her – desperation, grief, confusion – a veil had fallen, a wall been constructed. It nagged at him; but he had other things to think about. Every day, more desperately ill people appearing at the archway of the hospital entrance, and every day more bodies to transfer into the great mass grave, to be covered with quicklime and cold damp earth.

The day moved on. A good day for cleaning, for laundry, Margaret thought. A day without talking to anyone. She gathered together the bed-linens, a pile of clothing, the blue and white linen cloth from the table. Clouds moved across the sky; a chill breeze rustled through the dead leaves on the ground alongside the house. Sunshine streamed through the openings in the clouds, and then faded once again. The air was cool, but dry enough that the wash would be ready to be folded and taken inside before dusk. Each piece went into the washtub, and she scrubbed vigorously, more energetically than was really needed. And then another bucket of water heated on the stove, and one more shirt or pair of trousers or sheet scrubbed and wrung out and hung in the yard to dry. It was only when she was hanging the laundry that she thought again of Patrick, of Maureen, of the missing voices. We will make a plan, Charles Kingsbury had said. The plan must be mine, she thought to herself: I must take hold of where my life is leading. Not remain where I am not wanted.

The following morning she dressed carefully, and then sat with James. The boy swung his legs back and forth as he perched on the bench, his hands placed on either side of him along the plank. Yesterday he had gone to the field with Robert and Timothy, gathering the potatoes as they dug them from the ground. What was missing was play, was running after Maureen, playing tag, the certainty that she would then turn and run after him, her cries of delight when she caught up to him. He loved his mother, but his mother was not Maureen.

"James, I will not be gone long, and you can help them again this morning." She stroked his tousled hair: just a child, too young to burden with all the things that were on her mind. "When I come back we shall go for a long walk in the fields." She recalled another walk many years ago, with Annie, up the hill to watch the clouds. Back then, she was little more than a child, and the clouds and the stone walls and the affectionate horse along the way had helped to heal her own sense of loss.

Careful plans, she always made careful plans. Margaret drummed her fingers on the bare wood of the table. The blue and white cloth was folded neatly at the other end; she would not spread it out here again. The stack of books on the floor beside her chair – she must find a box for them, something to hold them for the journey.

At mid-day she returned to the house again. The conversation with Dr. Kingsbury had been careful, courteous, neither of them having anything new to say. She listened; he listened. But there were many long pauses, and no decisiveness on either side. When she reached the doorway of the cottage, she heard voices inside. At the table sat Robert and Timothy and James, and Deirdre stood pouring their tea. The talking stopped as she entered. Her pile of books had been pushed to the corner of the room, the blue and white tablecloth thrown on top of them.

Deirdre turned her back toward her, ignoring her presence; the two older boys lowered their heads awkwardly, uncertain of how to escape the crisis, the conflict at hand. No place had been set for her at the table.

"You can sit by me, ma," James said, breaking the silence of the moment.

Margaret took a cup from the shelf, sat down, and waited for tea to be poured for her. Everyone was as if frozen in stone. So she pulled the teapot toward her, and poured it herself.

"Potatoes still to be dug, Robert?" she asked, straining to ease the moment.

He nodded, still evading her eyes. Such confusion: Deirdre had said that Margaret would be gone, any day now, and the house would be rightfully his. What was he to do with a house? In truth it would be more Deirdre's than his own, and he and Timothy would become unpaid hired hands on his own farm. He boiled with resentment for his father Patrick's untimely escape. If only he would come back; or, if not him, at least Francis, who had gone off to distant adventures. Old enough to be a man, Deirdre had berated him earlier in the day, but he did not comprehend what she might be meaning by such words. He shifted on the bench, looking toward Timothy. They knew how to hoe the field, plant the potatoes, dig them up when the season ended. If he was a man, he would be going to the pub of an evening, lifting a glass and singing songs, not standing in the lane hoping for a glimpse of some lass whose name he did not even know.

There was bread on a plate on the table, just two or three slices left.

"Where is Pa? Why isn't he here?" Timothy's voice, seldom heard, seemed to come from another world.

Margaret looked steadily at him, setting down the slice of bread in her hand. The look about him was one of panic, not wanting to know something, not wanting to be told. If she said, he is dead, the look would be no less uncomprehending. Timothy the quiet one, always agreeable, always following in Robert's wake, now lost at sea, his anchor gone. She saw him with new eyes, a light cutting through the veil of her own sadness – three boys, none of them yet really men, all suddenly without the father who was their rock, their foundation. Patrick had been that for her for only these few years, but for them it was all they had known.

"Timothy," she said, looking at the boy. "I need a good sturdy box, not too large, but big enough to hold my books. They should not just sit on the floor. Do you think you could find one for me?"

He looked at her gratefully, nodding. That there was something for him to do must mean that life was continuing, that all was not lost.

Deirdre, still saying not a single word, pulled her chair back from the end of the table and cleared away the boys' dishes. She did not intend to leave the room while Margaret was still in it. Nor did Margaret plan to go anywhere. She refilled her cup with tea, and went to sit beside her pile of books, tumbled in disorder. Carefully she stacked them by size, the easier to pack them once a box had been found.

A shadow at the open door: once again Dr. Kingsbury. He nodded toward Deirdre and the others. Without even a word of greeting, he spoke directly to Margaret.

"Have you thought about my proposal, about what you are to do?"

She stood up, and took a deep breath. "I am planning to go to Dublin, to find work there, and a place to live. James will go with me. And I shall find some way for him to go to school." She shocked herself – the words came tumbling out of her, not anything she had thought about until that very moment, but all of a piece, like a revelation from on high. "Perhaps – there must be a hospital in Dublin where I can find work."

Everyone in the room was looking at her: she seemed so composed. None of them could hear the heart hammering in her ribcage.

Charles Kingsbury was the first to speak. "This will be a great loss for Roscrea. No doubt in my mind, you will find things to do there. I shall provide you with a letter of reference, and certainly George Powers would do so as well if you asked him. So many hospitals, a new one every few years, and every one of them desperate for staff. But are you sure you have decided to leave us? Certainly you could wait for spring," he added somewhat desperately. "The roads are deep with mud, and Dublin's streets are cold and dark in the winter. By May the days are longer, and your journey would be a less difficult matter."

Margaret was hardly hearing his words, barely seeing what was around her. "In January, early in the new year, is when I plan to leave. If you have someone new for the dispensary by then, I could help to train her. And Deirdre, the house will still be here for you to care for; do not concern yourself about it." She picked up the blue and white cloth, shook it our and refolded it, and placed it gently on top of the pile of books.

Charles Kingsbury looked bewildered, defeated. His shoulders sagged. Preparing for the chill outside, he pulled his cloak tighter, and donned his hat. He bowed his head, and turned toward the door.

DUBLIN, IRELAND

1833–1844

Shelter

FEBRUARY 1833

At the end of the journey, they stepped down from the carriage into an unfamiliar world. Noise, crowds, the sounds of people coughing, dogs barking. Even the air was different: gray, thick, with the smell of coal smoke and rotting garbage and open sewers. Their belongings were piled beside them: a wooden crate with books and blankets in it; a bundle of linens and Margaret's shawl; a satchel filled with all their other clothing. James stood wide-eyed, holding manfully to the handle of the satchel, determined to be his mother's protector just as Dr. Kingsbury said he should. Margaret held her head high, intent on appearing confident, whatever she might feel inside.

"Need help with your bags, missus?" A gravelly voice spoke from behind her shoulder. A short, stunted man in a cap, his grin almost a grimace, gripped the handle of a wheeled contraption, a wagon assembled from pieces found in the trash.

"No – yes – we must find a place to stay tonight." She tried to retain the appearance of knowing what she was about. The city was more than she had expected it to be: huge, intimidating, crowded, dirty. James was to be safeguarded, and herself as well.

The man, part elf, part demon, took hold of the bundle, and put his arm around James' shoulder. "A place to stay: that can be provided, and the morning will give other answers. Come along, now." He hoisted the wooden crate onto his wagon, and loaded the satchel beside it. "Not far: there is space for you for the night, for both of you, but what of the morrow?"

The day was fading, everything becoming dimmer, and the streetlights were not yet lit. She took James' hand, and they followed behind the cart. She spoke calmly, disguising inner turmoil. "A letter of introduction. I must go to Baggot Street in the morning. By tomorrow night I hope to have a position."

The man looked back at them skeptically. "A position, eh? Sure, there are lots of fancy houses welcoming ladies straight from the country like yourself. But hardly a place for a lad: if you care about him, better to have left him at home in the country."

She looked at him in some confusion. The city pressed in upon her, sounds, smells. They walked down a long street, and turned onto another, and then off that into a dark narrow lane, dirty, with refuse and animals underfoot. He stopped at a doorway halfway down. "Now my name, missus, is Matt Devan, and I do not know your name. But the house has many rooms, and the room my mother and sister share has space enough for you for the night. And two shillings would be reasonable for your accommodations." He extended an open palm, waiting. She fumbled in the depths of the pocket of her dress: not what she had expected to be doing, but then she had not really thought about what to expect.

Bells sounded, not far away: six o'clock, church bells, hanging above other sounds accumulated along the lane. The doorway was high: grimy gray stone framed it off from the brick wall, with a dirty window beside it curtained within by a ragged length of cotton. A cluster of children sat at the stoop, looking curiously at James, an unfamiliar boy in a place where familiarity was expected.

The hallway inside was cluttered, dark, with cracks of light at the edge of each door leading off it, muffled sounds on every side. They followed Matt Devan toward the back of the house, past the sagging stairway leading upward, until he reached yet one more door, rapped twice and pushed it open. More smells assailed them: the stale thick air of a space heated by a coal stove; the sharp sweaty odor of unwashed clothes; the sourness of old food left crusted in dirty pots. A flickering candle provided just enough light to see the two women – one old, immense, immovable, seated by the stove; the other short and angular, as peculiar looking as Matt Devan, leaning on a broom that seemed to be a support for her, almost like a crutch, rather than a tool for cleaning.

"An' who's this?" The old woman's voice issued a sharp challenge, and James moved a step closer to his mother, so that she was between him and the crone. Matt Devan dumped the wooden crate unceremoniously on the floor inside the door.

"Guests for the night, ma. Just off the stage from Tipperary, needing a place until the light of day. Nothing to fear – they will not be here long, and they pay. A letter of introduction, she says she has, and perhaps even tomorrow she'll have a position."

Even in the dark room Margaret could see Mona Devan's glittering eye. "A position, eh? She's a bit thin and bony for a fancy house, and looks to have airs ill-suited for kitchen help. Living as she has in the country, what would she be suited to do, may I inquire?" The sharp voice ended in a cackle, and she shifted her great bulk in her chair.

Margaret spoke in a low voice, not wanting to be drawn into an argument, but needing to reassure her reluctant hostess. "The letter is to the Matron at the City of Dublin hospital on Baggot Street. I am hopeful of getting work there."

"Mother of God, a hospital! You'd be better off in a whorehouse than a hospital! People dying every day, coughing, bleeding, shaking of the fever. What would possess you to choose such a place? And the boy: what will you do with him? For sure, the workhouse would be a better situation."

Through all this the younger woman had stood with her broom, without moving, simply watching the newcomers. Margaret looked toward her, uncertain what to say or do. Finally she plunged on: "I am Margaret Fogarty, and I do not know my way around the streets of Dublin. In the morning could you show me the way to Baggot Street?" The other woman continued to stare at her, and then nodded and set aside her broom.

"It's not far, indeed, mum. Whether it will be worth your walking there or not is hard to say, but I'll go there with you and lead you back again. And the boy: he can stay here or follow along, as you prefer."

The old woman spoke once again, in a less hostile tone. "Dora, offer the visitors a bit of tea."

"But we have no spare cups, ma." She looked around, distressed, as if they might appear from somewhere.

Margaret went to the wooden box, and loosened the wide leather strap that had kept it secure during the journey. "Cups we have, and blankets for the night. And James: in the top of the satchel is the rest of the bread from our travels, enough to share. Get it out now, and break it into good big pieces."

Mona Devan's voice took on a certain sweetness. "Bread, is it? It's been a week since we saw fresh bread. You're more than welcome, then, Margaret Fogarty, however long you may care to stay." She reached out her fleshy arm greedily. "Food comes and goes, and in between there's only the hunger and a bit of tea."

The bread went quickly, and the darkness thickened soon after. Margaret retrieved their blankets from the wooden box, and folded them to make a snug sleeping pallet for herself and the boy, away from the stove and against a wall behind the wooden box. As the stove cooled Mona nodded off to sleep, still seated in her chair, a worn coverlet tucked around her ample form. Matt Devan had gone out again, without a word, and Dora had made her own bed beside the pile of unfolded clothes, a buffer of insulation from the cold of the dirt-encrusted window. Soon the only sounds were Mona's rhythmic snoring and the skittering of small animals across the floor. James lay beside her, straight and still, barely breathing as he slept, afraid even to dream of what might happen next. Margaret closed her eyes.

It seemed only moments before she awakened, in the darkness before dawn, hearing Mona's breathing and a steady distant coughing from the room above them. No roosters crowed here in the city: wheels scraped on the cobblestones, against the measured clop-clop of horses' hooves. James was still beside her, still asleep, his small clenched fists against his eyes as if to protect himself from the sight of the world around him. He looked to be a little boy again, barely more than an infant. She tried to erase all the turmoil from her mind, to only think of protecting this her child, her only child.

As glimmers of light started to appear at the window she sat up, pulled on her clothing, combed her hair. She thought back to the things Charles Kingsbury had said to her: be clear about your skills, your experience, your time with George Powers and myself. She felt once again in her pocket for the precious letter.

When Dora was awake she stirred the coals in the stove, went out to the back yard to empty the chamber pot, and then to the lane to fill the teakettle, and brought it in and set it to heat on the stove. The room came to life: Mona complaining from her chair, making her way with her cane out to the cold back yard and then in again; Matt Devan pulling himself together and leaving with scarcely a word; James watching it all in quiet curiosity. After tea, Margaret could no longer contain her impatience to set out.

"As soon as you could free yourself, Dora, I should like to go to Baggot Street, if you are still willing to take me there. And James will come too: it will help him learn his way around." Dora looked confused, as if she had forgotten the evening's conversation, but then she nodded, and emptied her cup.

Dora drew her cloak around her shoulders and stood at the door of the room, ready to leave; Margaret rose to follow her.

"Come along, James. We have much to do today."

"Can't I stay here, ma? I want to play."

It had been a long time since the boy had spoken of playing; it tore at her heart.

"We will be back before long. Right now I want you with me, as we learn our way around the city."

Obedient, if reluctant, he climbed to his feet, and slipped his shoes on. She passed her hands over his tousled hair, willing it to a certain tidiness. They left the room, walked down the dark hallway and into the daylight. The cobblestones gleamed with the remaining moisture from the night's rain, which had washed the coal smoke out of the air. Dora led the way down one street and then another, turning corners, dodging horses and carriages, across a bridge over the river, past the great gate of the college, then left, then right, then left again. Soon they were in front of the long cream-colored building, with rows of windows on each of its three storeys, steps going up to its dark imposing double door, with two ornamental pillars on either side supporting a lintel beam inscribed with the words "THE CITY OF DUBLIN HOSPITAL." Dora stopped at the opening in the iron fence.

"There y'are, mum. Shall I wait for you here?"

"Would you want to come inside, Dora? It's cold here on the street."

"Never. A hospital is not a place I want to see the insides of. I'll be here when you're done, you can be sure."

Margaret put her hand on James' shoulder, and took him with her up the steps to the door. She pulled the bell chain; they heard its clang echo inside the building, and then footsteps on the floor coming toward them. The door opened, and the porter peered out at them, not speaking for a moment.

"Is the boy ill?"

"No – no," Margaret answered. "I have a letter - it is for the Matron, Clara Osgood. May I see her?"

The man extended his hand; she fumbled and drew the packet out from where she had it hidden in her dress pocket. He looked at it carefully, as if to convince himself that she was speaking the truth. Then he opened the door wider, motioned them inside, and closed it with a bang. He pointed wordlessly to the long bench along the wall of the entry hall, and disappeared into a dark corridor, his footsteps echoing as he walked its length, and then climbed up a stairway to the second floor.

Mother and son sat silently, absorbing the strangeness of the place, dark portraits in heavy frames barely visible among the shadows on the high walls. Margaret suddenly recalled the paintings hanging in the great rooms of Winston Court, ghostly presences in the rooms where she and her mother had swept and dusted. James had never seen such things. He gazed up at the faces, larger than life, forbidding, godlike. He wished that he were back in the lane, playing.

Now they heard another sound of footsteps, quicker, lighter, coming toward them. A woman appeared, clad in a dark gray dress, with a high white ruffled collar at her throat and a white cap perched on her hair.

"I would swear you are a gift from God," she said briskly, without even a word of greeting. "Less than a year we have been open, and already one of the ward nurses has been taken by the fever. Dr. Kingsbury writes such glowing words of you. But why do you find yourself here in Dublin?" She had a sharp, inquiring eye, and she looked Margaret and James up and down, to determine whether they were real flesh and blood or just a mirage.

Margaret folded her hands in her lap, and spoke softly but clearly. "When my husband and daughter died two months ago, both taken by the fever, I was suddenly without a home to call my own. Dublin seemed to offer the promise of work, at the very least, and I came with the hope that I would find a place to live, and a way for my son James to go to school." She took a deep breath and went on. "Both Dr. Kingsbury and Dr. Powers did their medical studies here in this city, and they spoke words of praise for this new hospital. And so I came here first, before looking anywhere else."

Clara Osgood judged people on her first impression of them, and she was usually right. Staffing a hospital was a game of chance: there were so many unpredictables to it. The most upright of young women might turn out to become faint at the sight of blood; the most experienced were likely to move on quickly to more sedate occupations. To find someone who knew something about the care of the sick was most unusual, not an opportunity to be ignored. And Dr. Kingsbury, she knew, did not utter words of praise lightly.

"We need a new ward nurse as soon as possible, and if you would take the position, your room would be ready for you tomorrow. It is just now being cleaned and scrubbed, and the old mattress is to be taken out and burned and a new one put in." She paused for a moment, taking her eyeglasses from her dress pocket, putting them on and looking calculatingly at James. "A hospital is a difficult place for a young boy to be living. He might be better off with some family members in the countryside. But if you wish, for the moment he could bed down in the sitting-room of your apartment, until you have made arrangements for him. Your pay will be adequate but not generous, and you will, of course, receive a ration of beer. The market is nearby, so you can get food supplies at a time when your ward duties permit." She remained silent for a few moments, and then spoke once again. "So, Mrs. Fogarty, will you be joining us tomorrow?"

Margaret nodded vigorously, and put her arm around James' shoulder. "It will please me very much. I will do my best, mum," she said earnestly.

The Children's Ward

On the following morning, Margaret and James led the way. Matt Devan pushed his wagon loaded with their goods along the route to Baggot Street. They walked as if this was already their city. As they had returned from the hospital the previous afternoon Margaret had stopped first at a bakery, then at a fishmonger's, buying and bringing back with them gifts that assured their welcome for the second night's stay in the dark, dank chamber. It was something to remember, the dark fetid room: the life she would not live, the place where James would not be trapped.

The steps up to the building on Baggot Street, leading to the hospital's great double doors, already seemed like home. A moment after she sounded the bell, the right side of the dark door swung open, and the porter once again stood there. This time he gave her a nod of recognition, and then he took some of the parcels from Matt Devan's hands.

He looked down at the young boy. "Master James, I am Tom, and you must call upon me with any questions that bother you. This is your home now, a strange home perhaps, but the start of a new adventure." The boy looked up, fascinated: someone knew he existed, after all. "And how old would you be now, a fine lad like you?"

James answered him directly, so pleased to have a question he could answer outright. "Seven going on eight, sir. And I know my letters and numbers, though I have not been to school."

"Much more to learn here than that, young man. I am sure you will be a great help to me."

The Matron's swift steps could be heard coming down the long hallway. "Ah, Mrs. Fogarty, good, good. And did I mention to you that your duties are in the children's ward? It is the smallest, but in some ways the most complicated duty. Broken bones in children may knit more quickly, but the fear, and the loneliness, can leave a different kind of wound. From what Dr. Kingsbury said in his letter, you may have just the right skills to make a success of such work." She took Margaret's arm, and led her back down the corridor and up the staircase. Tom the porter, and James, and Matt Devan followed behind in procession, each of them carrying their share of the bundles and the precious wooden box.

At the head of the stairs the hallway led on toward the children's ward, but before it was a rack along one wall holding small crutches of various sizes, some of them looking large enough only for a doll, others almost right for an adult. Across from the rack, a doorway opened into the two-room apartment that was to become Margaret's and James' home, the ward nurse's suite. The first chamber as they entered was the snug dark sitting-room, with a bench, a narrow bookshelf, a cushioned easy chair, and a table with a lamp; and beyond the sitting-room was the bedroom, its high window open to let in air, with light streaming in from Baggot Street. It was a good-sized room, with a bed and a chest of drawers, a wardrobe and a dressing table, a small mirror hanging above the table. Everything in the small apartment was so white, so clean: walls, furniture, linens. Even the dimness of the windowless sitting-room seemed light and bright, and cozy as well.

All of the parcels were now placed in a line on the floor of the sitting-room. The five stood silently for a moment, and then Tom was the first to speak.

"With your permission, Mrs. Fogarty, I shall take James along with me to get supplies. We won't be more than an hour or so, and this will give you time to unpack your belongings." Tom motioned to Matt Devan, and handed him some coins, as they headed toward the stairs, James skipping to keep up with the two men.

"Tom is a fine man; he will take good care of your boy," the Matron said to Margaret. "I shall come back here in a half hour, so that we can begin your duties in the ward. One of the surgeons, Mr. Morrison, will be here shortly, and I must attend to his cases first." She nodded, and smiled, and left the room. Margaret was alone. She took a deep breath, and looked around with pleasure at her new surroundings.

Just at eye level, inside the door of the bedroom, was a row of a half dozen pegs. On the first she hung her cloak, pulling down its folds so that it was straight and neat. Then she opened the doors of the wardrobe. Half of its width was shelving, and the other half a rod for hanging dresses and shirts. So much space, all her own, to do with as she pleased. She opened the wooden crate, and lifted her precious books and lined them up on the bookshelf. The blankets and coverlets she shook out and re-folded, placing them in a neat pile on the foot of the bed. The two cups and two plates, with the knives and spoons and forks, she carried back to the sitting-room and laid them on the table. And then she sat down, by herself, in her own sitting-room, with a bookshelf half full of books beside her; just sat in the chair, savoring the silence.

After a little while, a rap on the door, and the Matron appeared. "Now, to show you the rest of the hospital. You will be in charge here in this ward, but you must know where things are." She led her into the children's ward, with the beds lined up on each side of it. More than a dozen beds, less than half of them occupied; five boys, one girl, varying in size, each of them seeming to have broken an arm or leg.

"How do they come to be here?" Margaret asked.

"Children of servants of the hospital's patrons, mostly. Usually an accident – a fall, or run over by a carriage or horse, or some such thing. Once in a while, a child born lame or deformed, and one of our surgeons undertakes to improve upon a sorry situation. No one with contagious diseases – they go to the fever hospitals, not here. And not blindness or eye maladies – there are special places for such treatment." Clara Osgood raised the shades all the way on the windows at the end of the ward, and opened them a few inches to admit fresh air. "Sister Prudence Horner, who is the head nurse, will spend time with you later and instruct you about our procedures with patients. This is such a new hospital we are still learning about the best way to do things; and of course each surgeon, each physician brings his own opinions of just how things are to be done. But," she lowered her voice in a conspiratorial fashion, "Those gentlemen come for their visits and then leave, and it is left to us to see that things continue, day in and day out, in a manner that is sensible and best for the patients."

Clara Osgood turned and led Margaret toward the stairway. "Let us go down so that I can show you the location of all the departments. You will find your way around quickly, but we should make things as simple as possible. Laundry, kitchen, pharmacy, storeroom, " – the Matron listed all of the work areas in the lower reaches of the building, and then pointing in another direction – "Surgical theatre, offices, board meeting room, parlor," – Margaret's head was spinning: so much new to comprehend! Clara Osgood turned this way and that, and Margaret followed docilely, nodding as if it all made sense. A hospital like this, so grand, so complex, was so much more than just a clinic. They walked back and forth, opening and closing doors, peering into dark closets, nodding to cooks and laundry maids, then upstairs again by another stairwell and past the entrance-halls to the other wards.

"And here we are back again. And this," Clara gestured to the woman standing waiting for them, short and square and crisp in her prescribed costume, "Is Sister Prudence Horner, who will train you in the practices here at the hospital." She nodded to both of them and then turned and went her way, leaving them alone.

The two stood facing each other, taking stock, in a moment of awkward silence.

"Well, Mrs. Fogarty, and you are a Papist, is it? But no matter: so long as you are good at details, and follow instructions, that will be no barrier." Prudence Horner was not a person who was given to smiling, or to wasting words on pleasantries. She was shorter than Margaret by several inches, but Margaret sensed that she was being looked down upon, somewhat as a disapproving elder aunt might do. At least, she thought to herself, there will be a clarity in her directives, and I can simply follow them.

"First bathing the patients, then bandages. Everything to be done in its proper order." Prudence Horner led Margaret to a large closet beyond the rack of crutches, and opened the door. Inside were shelves filled with neat rolls of bandages, piles of folded towels, jars of ointments. The head nurse selected what she needed, and handed the armload of supplies to

Margaret. Then she walked along the aisle of beds with their painted metal bedposts to the one closest to the far window. A boy of about eleven laid there, almost motionless. As Sister Horner pulled back the covers Margaret could see the bandaged leg, a cast from above the knee almost to the ankle.

"And so, Martin, not too many days longer and we hope that you will be up and out of here." She was not trying to cheer him up: she was making a statement about efficiency.

A basin of warm water, a rough wash cloth, soap, a large towel. The nurse put them each to use as a tool, showing her expertise, the boy beneath her hands simply incidental to the task, He lay perfectly still, rigid, as if only a frightened observer to what was happening. Then Margaret took his hand and smiled at him, and that small part of him melted, and his eyes took on life as if coming back from the dead.

One child after another, each of them stiff and silent, softened as she greeted them, became young again as she touched them and spoke their name. Prudence Horner moved along, organized, methodical, through a checklist of duties and procedures. Margaret followed, nodding, observant, taking possession of the ward and gradually, bit by bit, of the hearts of the children.

At the end of the day, she laid out boiled eggs and bread and tea on the table in the sitting room. James had grown, changed, in the few hours with Tom, and words tumbled out of him about everything he had seen and done. Nothing would be the same again: he had entered a new world. Margaret gazed at him fondly: a whole child, with ruddy cheeks and sparkling eyes, no bones broken, nothing keeping him still and frightened.

"And the railway, ma. So much noise, and smoke. And crowds to watch the engine when it leaves the station." For the moment everything was new, exciting. Endless experiences lay before him.

City Streets

James kicked a pebble along in front of him as he made his way along Baggot Street toward St. Stephen's Green. He knew every building, every bump in the paving-stones. For the years since he and his mother had come to Dublin to live at the Hospital, he had followed this route at least once a day – first always with Tom, and now more frequently just by himself. Sometimes he was sent on an errand. On other occasions, he was following a magical journey in his imagination, counting his steps, being careful to avoid certain cobblestones that might transport him to the spirit world. His memories of meadows and the sweet smell of new-mown hay, of chickens in the farmyard, of muddy lanes between rough stone walls, had faded.

The city streets held the promise of adventure, even of danger. The noise of traffic – the clop clop of horses, the squeal of carriage wheels – was a counterpoint to the human voice: conversation, argument, the call of peddlers, snatches of drunken song heard from the open doorways of pubs. He had grown into all of it, no longer a country lad but a Dublin boy, aiming to become a man of the world.

On a good afternoon, one with a breeze and the glint of sun, after the rain had stopped, James walked along the glistening pavement next to the iron fence that bounded St. Stephen's Green. The pebble laid at his feet: every day he had the pebble with him, tracing his route into the city.

"Aye, boyo! Would you like a new suit of clothing and a fine pair of shoes? Easy work I have for you, and a good reward for your labor!"

He looked up at the man on the wagon calling down to him. At first he thought the man was Matt Devan, for he had a similar appearance of disarray; but the man was taller, and the wagon larger, and the accumulation of discards marked him as a tinker in all likelihood.

The man spoke once again. "Cleaning out the necessaries and the ash-pits is not bad work and it must be done. A few hours a day, that is all, and new clothing as a reward. Not to mention the wages, which are quite reasonable."

"I am just on an errand for my mum: bread and fish for supper." James cast his eyes in the other direction, toward the lush foliage on the Green. "Thank you sir, but leave me alone: I must do what she asks of me."

He walked faster, away from the man on the wagon, crossing the street quickly and going out of reach of the traffic. It was not a sense of imminent danger: a good part of him would love to flee from the predictable, the daily errand for bread and fish and eggs and tea. He looked with yearning at the military uniforms that appeared along the streets – costumes that promised deliverance from the ordinary, the boredom of safety. To go to sea, to join the Queen's regiment – those were ways to get a new suit of clothing, and adventure as well.

At the end of the Green, he turned down Grafton Street, eyeing the people along the walkways more than the shop windows. And then past the College gate, and on across the bridge over the River Liffey, shadowing two soldiers in fine uniforms, straining to lengthen his stride to match with theirs. He was growing taller; his ruddy cheeks and tousled hair and ready smile promised that he would be a fine-looking young man before many years passed.

"What will you be wanting?" The voice across the counter in the bakery broke into his daydream.

"A loaf, please, and two currant scones." He pulled the coins from his pocket, and picked up the bread and rolls wrapped with paper and string. The woman nodded brusquely and turned to the next customer as he went out the door.

The market was always crowded, with smells as well as with people. He pushed his way through the aisle, first for the smoked fish, then the butter – each parcel tucked together under one arm, leaving the other hand free for pulling out the coins. And then into the fresh air, free from the pungent stale odors, and on to the tea shop: the most precious packet of all, a tin of dry black fragrance, the sacred drink of every day's ritual. It was for this more than anything that Margaret was waiting.

And again, kicking before him, the pebble: back across the Liffey by a different bridge, wending his way south and east toward Baggot Street, the small stone skipping along and bouncing against curbs and over cobbles, avoiding the puddles in which it would be lost and drowned, until he reached the Hospital steps where he kicked it expertly to one side, to its secret resting place beside the fence, where he, James, would retrieve it once again to accompany him on tomorrow's errand.

If only there were someone to kick a ball with, to run races, play tag. All the children in the Hospital were invalids in the ward: Margaret was the only nurse with a child of her own. And at school – several boys near his own age sitting before the stern eye of the school-master, a crabbed old man hired by a surgeon to assure that his servant's children would have useful work skills – play never entered into what they were there for. Play was something he did only by himself, in his daydreams, kicking a pebble that skipped on before him.

Margaret spent her days, almost entirely, inside the building. Each morning she pulled back the curtains on the large window in her chamber, and opened the window wide, and breathed deeply. This was her encounter with the outside world. On Sundays, if no patient was in a crisis that demanded her presence at the bedside, she left the building for a few hours – to put on her bonnet, kneel for a while in a church, and walk the bridge across the river and back again, perhaps with cakes for tea. But aside from that she lived inside, caring for the sick and the injured, keeping everything in order, cherishing her tranquility and the comings and goings of her son James.

"Old enough to be in service or learning a trade, the boy is." Prudence Horner had a daily refrain, after she had reviewed with Margaret the new arrivals in each hospital ward, the particular concerns about each patient, the instructions left behind by surgeons and physicians on their regular visits. Margaret was still ward nurse for the children's ward, but she was more than that as well. Prudence Horner was feeling her age and becoming more cantankerous about dealing all the time with the ailments of others. Regularly she would make mention of her brother's cottage in Wicklow, the beauty and quiet of the hills and fields.

"So how much longer will the boy be staying here and eating all your bread and drinking your tea?" Each question drew Margaret into the inevitable defensive response, and then a quick changing of the subject to something else, some question about bandages or poultices or medicines.

On her Sunday walks, every street crowd had its men in uniform, sailors, soldiers, the embellishment of the crowds of humankind out taking the air. They called back the memories of her father, always standing a bit straighter when he donned his red coat. If James went walking with her, she felt the magnetism that the costumes had for him, turning their wearers into something more than mere men. In her mind she pulled him back, prohibiting him from ever departing from her side. He was hers, not free to become one of the wild geese. She knew he would never leave her.

Each day, following the pebble, James dreamed dreams. Once he went with Tom, out of the city and all the way to Dun Laoghaire to fetch a parcel from the docks at the harbor. He saw for the first time the ships with the tall sails, anchored off shore, awaiting the calming of the seas so that they could set off again for distant places. At that moment he lost his heart to the thrill of adventures far away. This was his secret, that he did not tell his mother; he did not even tell Tom, though Tom had his suspicions. But nothing was said, ever.

On Monday morning Clara Osgood would always appear at the door of Margaret's room, rapping lightly, entering when the door was opened to her, exchanging pleasantries. James made it a point to have left before she came.

"Nurse Horner will be leaving, a fortnight hence." The Matron had barely given a nod of greeting on the morning she made this announcement. Nurses came and went, as frequently as passing clouds; but Prudence Horner had been there since the hospital opened, as long as Clara Osgood herself.

Margaret caught her breath, uncertain what was the proper thing to say. She knew that the Head Nurse had always felt a certain coolness toward her, though she was civil and proper. Prudence Horner preferred to have nurses under her supervision who had no other attachments, people like herself. That Margaret was widowed, that she had a son, a boy rapidly growing toward manhood – these were impediments, however flawless her performance might be otherwise. That she learned quickly, did her tasks meticulously, made sick children comfortable, all these were less consequential than that she had other attachments than her work.

"It is the right time for her to retire, and so she will be leaving very soon to live with her brother's family in County Wicklow. A great loss for us, of course," the Matron continued, "But we have decided that you would be quite capable of taking her place."

Margaret was taken aback. "I am not sure – this is such a surprise, and I do not know if I have enough training. But I would like it very much."

Clara Osgood smiled. "You will be fine. All of the physicians and surgeons think highly of you, and of your ability to learn new things. Now," she said briskly, "There will be a few changes. First: we will want to have the Head Nurse rooms cleaned and painted when Sister Horner leaves, of course. And second: we have decided that you should be sent for midwifery training at the Rotunda, at the lying-in hospital. We have not had a properly-trained midwife on staff, and it would be an advantage both for us and for yourself. So this will be a time of transition, and we all will do our best." She smiled, and extended her hand, as if to an equal; and Margaret reached out, hesitantly, with her hand as well.

The following weeks were a blur. Her head was spinning, with new things to think about, new skills to master. The one thing that was constant, unchanging, was James, the one person in her life who had nothing to do with the hospital routine. His schooling progressed; and then, thanks to Tom's watchful eye, an opportunity was found, and he began to learn a trade – something very useful, as apprentice to a harness-maker. Each morning he would disappear, and then return at the day's end, carrying bread and fish and sometimes cheese.

A part of her knew that he grew taller from month to month, but certainly not older, she told herself. There were evenings when he spoke of ships, of the things that he had seen when he went to the wharves with Tom. She would nod and smile, hearing but not hearing.

Another winter and summer passed, and then another; and then one day Clara Osgood appeared in the hallway quite unexpectedly, looking a bit different from her usual placid self.

"Margaret. Two young men are in the parlor, coming, they say, from Roscrea, and asking for you."

Margaret followed her down the stairs, smoothing her apron against her skirt with her hands. Roscrea seemed so far away: its wounds had almost healed, and she did not know what visitors she would find.

In the parlor, sitting nervously on the edge of a bench, were Robert and Timothy, unmistakably the same people, even if older, more doleful, than she remembered.

"What a surprise!" she said warmly, disguising her own anxiety. "What brings you to Dublin?" The two boys – young men now – had risen to their feet, uncertain what to say. It was Timothy who finally gathered his wits about him and spoke up.

"Deirdre told us to leave, that there was no life for us there. And that you would have money for us, money from our father, to go to America." He stopped; he had nothing more to say.

Margaret was frozen in place, her mind racing. "To America! What a thought. There is no money, Robert, Timothy; and no place for you to stay here. What a strange woman she is. And Dublin is a hard place, full of people suddenly arrived from the countryside. Now let me think." She stood for a moment, recalling her own arrival in the city, now several years in the past, with little more than the young men had brought with them. "Wait here; I will be back in a little while."

She went off in search of Tom, the dependable solver of problems. He was in the storeroom, stacking boxes just arrived.

"Tom. Two young men from the country, from my late husband's family: I don't know what will become of them. They are farm boys, new to the city streets. Just like so many others." She looked at him, perplexed. When she had come to the city, her hope had hung on this possibility, here at the hospital, and the skills she had brought with her. Here on Baggot Street there were no potatoes to be hoed, no fields to be planted.

"So many others. If they can find a place to stay, perhaps they could find day labor as roustabouts at the docks. Not an easy life: people dream that the city will be an easy place."

As they stood there, James appeared at the door. His mother turned to him. "James. Robert and Timothy are here, from the family in Roscrea. Would you take them to Matt Devan's place, and see if they can arrange to stay there for a few days." She reached into her apron pocket, and pulled out a few coins. "This should help; and when they have left their belongings, bring them here again, for Tom to talk with them. And give them some advice."

She went back to the parlor, James following behind her. "You remember James, your young brother," she said to the other two. "Go with him now, and once you have found a place to stay, come back to see me once again." She bowed her head to them, and turned, and went back up the stairs.

Opening Doors

She had always lived here, it seemed. The building on Baggot Street was her whole universe, and every hallway and doorknob and bedpost was a piece of her domain. Others might come and go, but Margaret would be here forever, and happily so. She and Clara Osgood had partitioned this world, each of them ruling over its different kingdoms. James was her link to the outside, and she heard of its affairs from him, but thought little of what happened beyond the hospital doors.

The men who came to see patients, the physicians and surgeons, thought of the place as their hospital, and she nodded at their every word; but they were there only briefly, and when they left the wards and the patients were hers again, to care for and cherish and oversee.

Sometimes there would be visitors from afar – London, Edinburgh, Paris – wanting to know about surgery and treatments and therapies that were new to them. She dealt with all the newcomers evenly, answering their questions, trying not to be impatient about the invasions into her routine. After all, she knew more than anyone else about the place.

"Someone to see you in the parlor, mum: a physician, an older man, from the south. County Cork, if I am not mistaken." Tom came with the message and then went back down the stairs.

She finished what she was doing, and changed to a fresh apron, tucking loose hairs into the brim of her cap. Strands of grey lightened her brown tresses; she kept it neatly pinned into a knot at the back of her neck, where it would not be a distraction. As she walked toward the parlor, the voice she heard speaking with the Matron sounded oddly familiar.

"Margaret. I believe you may know Dr. George Powers."

He was an old man, standing there before her, but very much the same person. She might not have known him if they had passed on the street. She felt a child again, sitting in his study with a pile of books.

"A wonderful surprise." She tried to compose herself. "And Mrs. Powers and Lady Amelia – are they in good health?"

"Elizabeth sends you her regards. And my mother died several months ago, quietly and peacefully." He smiled, looking at Margaret, the girl he had first turned toward nursing. "It was quite curious: in the last few years, her memories of you played tricks on her, and she spoke of you almost daily. You seemed to have become, in her mind, the daughter she wanted and never had. And she gave instructions that this should be given to you." It was a small purse, decorated with silver-grey beading. Margaret remembered it, something that Lady Amelia often had with her, to which she had some special attachment. She had never seen her take anything out of it: it had simply seemed to be one of her treasures, laden with distant memories.

"She thought you might make use of this some day, if you were to start over in life." The bag was heavy, strangely weighty for the smallness of its size. She held it for a moment in her hands, and then untied the knot that held it closed, and looked inside it. The purse was filled with coins – large, heavy ones, not the kind she was used to handling; English coins, more of them than she had ever seen together at one time.

"Think of it as an inheritance: something that will open doors for you," George Powers was saying. "It is not an enormous amount, but if you put it to good use, you will be fulfilling my mother's wishes."

She stared at him, first silently, and then she murmured, "Thank you, thank you." After another silence, she said, "Sometimes it is easier when there is no way to open doors. This will give me much to think about."

Dr. Powers rose from chair where he had been sitting, and put his hands on her shoulders. "You are a fine woman, Margaret, and you have made us proud. Dr. Kingsbury feels just as I do, that you are a model for the nursing profession. If only we had a hundred more of you. Wherever you go, you will make your mark." He picked up his hat, and bowed gravely, and left the room.

The small purse, beaded and be-ribboned, was too fanciful for her wardrobe or belongings; but it brought to mind clearly the image of Lady Amelia with her crystal and porcelain. Margaret clutched it under her arm as she climbed the stairs and walked the hallway, and stood undecided at the entrance to her room. Then she moved to the far wall, and removed the cloth that covered the wooden crate, still with her, once the container of books and now the place to store bits of her past. The old shawl was there, and the tiny velvet-covered box holding the brooch. She laid the purse down beside the small box on the bottom layer, and folded the shawl on top of it, and closed the crate again, smoothing the cloth back in place. She could not think quite yet about the contents of the purse, and whether it really belonged to her. Too much might change. She adjusted her apron, re-tied the apron-strings, and set out to do her daily rounds of the wards.

Late in the day, Clara Osgood stopped at the door of her sitting-room, a questioning look on her face.

"Dr. Powers: is he a good friend of yours?"

"When I was a girl, I was in service in his house."

"In service, nothing more?"

"His mother, Lady Amelia, was my special charge, and she now just recently died. He brought a small memento she had left for me, an embroidered purse she often carried with her. I am very moved that she still had me in her thoughts, after all these years. It must be more than twenty years since I had seen her – she was very old by the time she died."

The Matron appeared to relax a bit: she had been quite tense when she came to the door, as if anticipating bad news.

"So. I feared that he might be coming to take you away from us."

"No, no. He was very good to me, and gave me the wish to become a nurse, to be what I am today." Margaret smiled. "I have come a long way since my days at Winston Court. Lady Amelia – I would not say she loved me, but she considered me her own, her possession." Nothing more was said, or needed to be said: things would continue in their customary fashion.

Margaret could not come and go in her own quarters without an awareness of the new presence. She would sense a kind of heat emanating from the small parcel buried deep in the wooden crate. Could others feel it too, she wondered. James came and went as always, oblivious of everything, even of her, it seemed. He was taller, older, moodier; he had dreams not told to her or to anyone, and a growing anger, almost a rage, with the fear that his dreams would never come true.

She knew he saw the other brothers, Timothy, Robert. He said nothing, but at times he came home with a particular scowl, as if he had been in an argument and come out second best. She was relieved that he said nothing to her about it – better that it be just between them, whatever set them on edge. Perhaps just the drink; perhaps the hopelessness, the absence of any brighter future.

Then one night he came into the room, still looking belligerent but as if he had made up his mind about something.

"I need a different life, ma. To go to sea, or better, to join the army. There is nothing for me here. The other two, they're turning into nothing at all. I need to escape." His eyes looked at her, almost pleading: he did not want her tears, her protestations.

She held her peace, kept herself calm: she did not want to drive him into something.

"Why not America?" she asked. "That would be a better life."

He looked at her with exasperation. "And who's to pay the passage, ma? Not that it's so much, but I have nothing. And the same with Rob and Tim: had we the money, we'd go in a minute. Ships there are aplenty, and broadsheets posted on every wall advertising their departure. But it isn't free, and our pockets are empty." He fell silent.

She sat, thinking, her hands folded in her lap. "The money can be found," she said finally. "Speak to the others, and then find a departure a month hence. A sturdy ship, be sure it is seaworthy; and for the four of us – I shall leave as well. From here, to some place that will lead us to New Haven: that is where Francis and the others from Roscrea settled, from what I hear."

He looked at her unbelievingly. "You would leave all this? Such a good position you have, and they need you."

"What I need is for you to have a life: nothing here is worth more than that." She looked at him unflinchingly. "Now go: see what you can find about departures."

NEW HAVEN, CONNECTICUT

1844–1868

Starting Over

SEPTEMBER 1844

The earth seemed to be moving rhythmically beneath her feet. For seven weeks, almost all of the time since she had boarded the ship at Dublin, she had been at the mercy of the sea. Up and down, sometimes gently, often with the violence of the ocean storms: it had become as natural as breathing. Now Margaret was trying to readjust to life on land once again. She stood at the roadside, just where the Long Wharf met the land, and looked northward toward the buildings of the city. Tall steeples were silhouetted against the sky; beyond them was a high ridge with red rocks on it, as if marking the border of this particular world. When she looked back along the wharf into the harbor, she saw sloops and sailing ships, flags fluttering in the breeze. Teams of horses stood patiently as barrels and boxes and bundles were off-loaded from shipboard and piled onto wagons of various sizes.

Her belongings were laid out beside her: no place for them to go, at least not until Robert and Timothy returned. It was only a half hour since they had left.

"Is your husband with you, ma'am?" The driver stood beside his wagon, waiting for the loading to be finished. He did not mean to be forward; he could tell she was Irish, just from looking at her, and thought a friendly word might be welcome. "I came myself from Cork, some years ago. A long and difficult journey: I remember it too well."

She did not want to seem too familiar, but there was no harm in some small talk. "My husband is long dead. My sons and I just arrived, from New Brunswick, after the ocean voyage."

"And how many sons do you bring with you?"

"Two," she said softly. "There was a third, but the ship fever took him, just a month ago." She could not bear to think about it.

"May he rest in peace," he said sympathetically, touching his hand to his cap. "It's a hard, cruel life, missus, even here in America."

Despite all the comings and goings along the waterfront, the place seemed tranquil and orderly compared to Dublin. The same had been true in St. John in Canada, their first landfall, and then in Boston, where the packet-boat had stopped for a day to offload and to await the various parcels to be carried on south along the coastline. Except for the first few hours out of New Brunswick, the sea had been calm, and the coastline visible toward the west for most of the journey.

She had felt herself to be imprisoned in a dark cave since James had sickened and died, the fever carrying him away in less than two days. Almost twenty had died during the voyage – "Not a bad number," she heard one of the crew say cheerfully. She had stood frozen, Timothy and Robert on either side of her, as the captain read a prayer and the blanket-wrapped body of the boy, her heart's true love, was cast over the rail into the roiling grey waters.

After Boston, as the small ship rounded the Cape and continued south and west, she began to feel a glimmer of light in her life once again, not that she expected that real brightness would ever return. And now on land, she waited for the next chapter.

The driver had been piling boxes and bundles in place, securing them with heavy rope, shifting the goods until they seemed balanced and steady. Before he mounted the driver's seat, he came over to Margaret once again.

"Every hour or two I come by this way. If I can be of assistance, just keep an eye out for me." He tipped his cap, and flicked the whip above his team. She said nothing, but smiled. Her wooden crate would be a comfortable enough seat while she waited.

The scrap of paper with the address on Morocco Street was all the information she had, and she had given it to Robert when the two brothers set off on their search. How many years ago was it, that the two or three letters had come from Francis to the family in Roscrea? At least a decade, she calculated: before Patrick died, before she had gone with James to Dublin. He might not be here; he might not even be alive. But they had to start somewhere.

A stew of smells assailed her: smoke from a factory beyond the wharf; the sweat of horses, and the pungent manure dropped along the roadway; the sharp briny salt air blowing in off the Sound. She wanted nothing more of the sea. While on the ship crossing the Atlantic the quarters had been so cramped, the ceiling not even high enough to stand up straight. Within a few days of leaving Dublin the smell of illness and death had pervaded the hold. It was easy to believe what was whispered, that the same ship had carried slaves from Africa to the Americas, human beings chained together to keep them from jumping into the sea, chained together whether alive or dead. For her it had also been a nightmare: resolutely she pushed it from her mind, but it returned again and again, each time catching her off-guard.

People kept passing on the road – almost all of them men, leading horses, carrying tools, walking purposefully and taking no notice of her. Would she recognize him, she wondered, if Francis were one of them. How tall was he? Would his eyes still have a certain gleam that she remembered, or was that simply imagined? He was older than Robert and Timothy by some years, and just barely older than herself. She closed her eyes for a moment and tried to see him once again, and only a shadowy image came to her. What was he now, she wondered: still a blacksmith? Or perhaps something more – more prosperous – a breeder of horses, like Patrick had been, putting to use all he had learned from him. And then suddenly she thought: perhaps married, with a wife and children. No reason not to be, here in a new world.

The walk away from the waterfront had taken Robert and Timothy into unknown territory, streets lines with trees and houses, with horses tied to hitching-posts before many garden gates. Between the two of them, they had little idea of where they were going, and, as usual, Robert took the lead. Morocco Street, the slip of paper said. After the gracious white houses close to the Green, the streets changed, and the buildings became smaller and more ramshackle, their entryways closer to the roadway, and few of them with any evidence of a garden.

"Are you sure this is the way?" Timothy felt disoriented in the best of circumstances. He still sensed the earth swaying beneath his feet, as the ship's deck had for so many weeks. Robert plodded ahead, past gentlemen and urchins, looking for any sign of kindred beings, people of his own kind, to whom he could even direct a question. An old man stood beneath a tree, smoking a pipe, looking curiously at them as they approached. Robert pulled the slip of paper from his pocket and unfolded it, showing it to him.

"So, Irish, are you?" The man looked them up and down, after he saw the address. "The town's full of 'em already, and now here's two more." He took his pipe from his mouth, spat on the ground, and waved dismissively in the direction they were already heading, northwest from the waterfront. "Morocco Street: every room in every building, they're packed up to the rooftop. You'll know you're there when you get there."

So they went along further, another ten minutes, and suddenly, although they were in a new land, there was something of home about it. A touch of brogue in the voices, a certain air of welcome and friendliness; a drunk sprawled at the roadside, a man and woman locked in argument. It was not Dublin, or Roscrea, but it was something of both of them at the same time.

"*Morocco Street*" the sign at the corner said, and they walked the length of the first block, and then the second, not sure what would give them the clue that they were at the right place. Just beyond the second corner was a saloon, its door ajar, two men about their own age standing just outside. They looked to be avoiding something: work, perhaps; going home, just as likely. The drink was in them, but not so much that they would take offense at a question.

"Can you tell me: do you know Francis Fogarty, living on Morocco Street?" Robert spoke to the two, who swayed a bit as they tried to focus on his face and his words, spoken in something of an unfamiliar accent.

"There's Fogartys what come and go. Ask at the church: the Father kin tell ya everyone, and where they might be staying. Nobody's in the same house two months in a row. The church and the saloon – those are the places to find someone. And he ain't here, at least not today." He guffawed, proud at his own attempt at a joke: it was not often that anyone would stand and listen to him.

"And where's the church?" Timothy looked around distractedly, not sure he would know what one looked like.

The second man waved his arm vaguely. "Down there a ways – brick, and with a sign and a big wooden door. Go ask at the house beside it: the priest should be there, if he's not off burying somebody."

They trudged on for a few minutes more, passing strangers, faces who looked at them with idle curiosity, seeing little promise in them. More newcomers, expecting a better life.

The church was not large, but enough different from the neighboring buildings that they found it quickly. The house beside it was plain, austere, lifeless: perhaps deserted. They knocked at the door. After a minute's silence they heard footsteps, and the door opened.

"Yes?"

The man in the doorway was lean, worn-looking, with thinning hair. But his eyes looked at them, not past them, and he seemed ready to hear them speak.

"Father. We're here just off the boat from Dublin, and looking for Francis Fogarty. Do you know of him?" Robert tried not to seem too anxious about what the answer might be.

"Frank Fogarty. Not much of a church-goer, if I remember rightly." He stifled a smile. "He was here for a number of years, but I recall that he left perhaps three years back. What brings you here looking for him?"

"He's kin, Father, and we're looking for a place to stay, for work. His is the only name we know."

"Just the two of you, eh?"

"And also my father's widow. She's waiting with the baggage, down near the water." They stood, waiting, feeling helpless and lost.

Father Matthew Maguire had this conversation over and over again: people arrived, thinking that everything would be clear and simple. Not that the men would have any difficulty finding work – any man who could stand on his own feet could find a job in two or three days. But a place to live, especially with a widow trailing along with them – that was not so easy.

"And where's your home, may I ask?"

"Roscrea, County Tipperary, Father. For four years past we've been in Dublin, but life in Ireland is hard – hard to find work, hard to keep from going hungry most of the time."

"Come in, come in. I'll give you the address of a rooming-house that's not too disorderly. You should be safe there, until you get your bearings." He scribbled it on a scrap of paper: John Sullivan, 43 Morocco Street. "They should know more of Francis Fogarty and his whereabouts. He's not in New Haven now, of that I'm quite sure."

He showed them to the door. "Now don't forget Mass on Sunday: nine o'clock. And confession the day before, mind you."

He showed them out, and they started down the street again, back the way they had came. Number 43 was a substantial house, with a porch on the front. One of the porch steps was broken, listing lower at one end, and the shutters on the parlor window were hanging askew. But a man was sitting on a chair on the porch, as if expecting them.

"Mr. Sullivan?"

"Who wants to know?"

"I'm Robert Fogarty, sir, and this here's my brother Timothy. We're just arrived, and needing a room."

"Just the two of you?"

"And one more as well."

"I've a room, but it's small for three, And I need a week's rent paid in advance. Have you the money?"

"I do, for the week; and we will be looking for work on the morrow."

He took them inside, and up the stairs. He was right: it was a small room, but not dark and dank and squalid like their quarters had been in Dublin. A breeze blew in the windows, catching the curtains. Two beds would do fine: one for the two of them, and one for Margaret.

Robert reached into his pocket for the coins Margaret had given him, and fumbled as he counted out the unfamiliar currency. They had changed money in Boston, but it was still something he had to squint at to see what was in his hand. He handed over the amount requested – one, two, three – and they shook hands.

They set down their packs. "We'll be back again in a half hour." He nodded, handed them the key to the room, and led them back down the stairs. Once again he took his seat on the porch.

When they reached the waterfront, Margaret was still seated on the wooden crate, talking once again to the man who had befriended her earlier.

"Did you find Francis?"

"He's not here, they say. But we have a place to stay, for the first week, at least."

"My husband's sons – Robert, Timothy. Both of them blacksmiths."

The teamster nodded to them genially. "Tell me where you'll be staying, and I'll carry the baggage there for you." He hefted the crate and the bundles onto the wagon, and helped Margaret up to the seat beside him. It was a small thing indeed he was doing, but he remembered how much such small things could mean in a strange new place. He picked up the reins and started up away from the wharf, with the two men following along side. For Margaret it was her first view of the town. She saw what Robert and Timothy had seen, but other things as well: no beggars; no children in rags. As they neared Morocco Street, she saw a large grey building with substantial columns along its front façade, set back from the road, with a horse grazing in the field in front of it.

"And what is that?" she asked curiously.

"The State Hospital, they call it. For sick people, they say, but most would rather stay at home and be cared for by their own. It's been there a few years now, and hardly anyone in it. They even rent out space for storage, I hear."

It was hard for her to imagine an almost-empty hospital. The memories of her wards in Dublin flooded into her mind, and she felt tears welling up. Oh, how she missed that ordered familiar world. She pushed from her mind the thought that she never should have left.

When they reached 43 Morocco Street, they lifted their belongings down and placed them on the porch, and then each reached up and gave Margaret a hand as she jumped down.

John Sullivan stared at them. "You didn't say you had a woman with you."

"Margaret Fogarty, my father's widow." Robert presented her.

"And a widow, at that: nothing but idle talk, and eating up whatever money you think you can bring home." Mr. Sullivan had clear opinions on the matter.

Margaret spoke up. "I shall not be here long, sir. I have other plans." She smiled rather coolly. Suddenly exhaustion overwhelmed her. Sleep was all she wanted. She followed the two inside and up the stairs.

Morocco Street

Early the next morning, when Margaret awakened, she could hear the sound of rain whispering against the window-pane. The other two lay sprawled and sleeping soundly on the bed. The grey sky, the green maple leaves starting to yellow, the streaks of rain etching the glass: she was in to a new place, where no one knew her, where she might even become a different person. The question of Francis, of where and who he might be, was still unresolved. But here she was, with the sea-passage paid and behind them, in a safe dry room. The coins were still in the purse buried deep in the crate, hidden beneath her carefully folded nurse's garb.

She rose and dressed quietly, leaving the room carrying only a cup and a small tin of tea leaves. She could hear others stirring throughout the house: surely the stove was hot in the kitchen, and the kettle might be boiling. She walked down the staircase, and back along the hallway to the kitchen.

The fire in the stove was burning, and the steam from the kettle filled the air with its warm moisture. Someone was sitting beside the table, a paring-knife in her hand, a bowl of apples in front of her. She was a short round person, with ruddy cheeks and wispy hair, and intent on her task. The sliced apples were piling up in a bowl, and the peels and cores lay in a heap in front of her. The crust was already spread in the pie-pan.

"May I take some water for tea?"

"Of course, of course. And you're the new one: himself said there was a woman in the room, nothing more than that. What brings you here, to New Haven of all places? Hardly paradise, I hope you know."

She had a brisk, precise manner about her: place an apple just so, quarter it, deal with the peel and core of each quarter, then slice it evenly into the bowl. Eight good-sized apples, each of them perfect in form and dappled red and green, had stood in a line before her, and now she was halfway through the line.

"I am Elizabeth Sullivan, Betty to you. Mr. Sullivan is in charge, but I actually run things here." Her voice dropped to an almost-conspiratorial whisper. Margaret sensed that there was a perpetual familial skirmish, that each would have a different account of the events of the day, of the pros and cons of any issue, probably even of the weather.

Margaret filled her cup, and took the seat at the other side of the table to which Betty Sullivan had gestured. The shelves behind her along the kitchen wall were filled with foodstuffs: canisters of flour and sugar and salt, all appropriately labeled; jars of preserved fruits and vegetables and jams. She felt almost ill surrounded by such an abundance of things to eat.

Betty reached into the bread-box, pulled out a loaf and cut a generous slice, put it on a plate with a spoon beside it and a jar of plum preserves, and pushed it toward Margaret without a word. Margaret stirred uncomfortably: did she take her for a charity case?

"We came here because – someone we knew lived in New Haven, and we hope to find him." For the moment, that was as much as she wanted to say.

"Myself now, I was born here." Betty dumped the bowl of apple slices into the pie crust, and sprinkled it with sugar and spice. Then she shook flour onto the board in front of her, pulled a ball of dough from another bowl, and began to roll it out on the board with a rolling-pin. "When Mr. Sullivan came off the boat, he seemed such a dashing figure." She rolled her eyes. Not that she planned to recite the whole story to every newcomer; just a hint was enough. "And who is the person you're hoping to find?"

"Francis Fogarty is his name. From my husband's family, you see; and it is some years since we've heard from him."

"Ah, yes, I remember him. Sitting on the stoop and talking with Mr. Sullivan – listening more than talking, it seems to me – and when he had something to say it was usually about horses. A blacksmith, isn't he? He went off from here maybe three or four years back, following someone who was breeding race-horses and had bought some land, some rich man with more money than sense. Off to someplace in New York State north of Albany – I think the name is Saratoga. People go there for the baths – people who have the time and money to do such things. Nothing more I've heard of Frank Fogarty since he left, but Mr. Sullivan may know more than I do."

She cut the pie crust rolled out on the board into strips, and began to weave a lattice across the top of the mounded apples, with bits of the fruit showing through as an added enticement. And then the edge of the bottom crust was folded over the ends of the strips, and crimped in place, and pressed down with the tines of a fork, straight even lines as a final bit of decoration.

"So." She rose from the table, opened the oven with a folded towel, slid the pie onto the shelf, closed the door with a thud, and sat down again. "And will the young men be supporting you, do you think? Or has any of that even crossed their minds?" It was a blunt question, not spoken rudely, but a bit intrusive. Margaret sensed that it was a gesture of friendship, however she might respond. Betty continued. "There's no shortage of work, you know: cleaning, or housemaid, or nursemaid, or cook. Not that it pays anything much to speak of, and most let you know what they think of the Irish even before you open your mouth. But it's often better than staying home and dealing with the laundry of two lazy young louts."

Margaret started to spring to their defense; but they were, after all, still asleep, and the day was moving on. The rich smell of the pie was filling the kitchen, and soon it would reach the other rooms of the house.

"Do you know anything about the hospital?" she asked. "In Dublin, that was my work, as nurse in a hospital."

"Is that so, now? Well, the place hasn't amounted to much. A big fancy building like that, but most people will stay and die in their own bed if they have the choice. Who works there, I am not sure, or what they do with themselves. Better to find yourself a position in some fine house not far from the Green, where you'll have a snug room of your own up under the eaves."

"And how would I set about locating Francis Fogarty, do you think."

"Best to have a word with the priest, and even with Mr. Sullivan as well. People come and go, and the word travels with them. You may never hear of him again, but people show up when you least expect them. Even," she said darkly, "When you least want them to."

The pie's aroma was mouth-watering, coloring the air. Betty opened the oven door an inch or two, peered in, and closed it once again. She wiped the table clean, and laid a bread-board down on it, and then pulled the pie from the oven and set it on the board with a flourish. And then she pulled a stew-pot from the shelf, and poured water into it and put it atop the stove. Then she picked up another knife and started in again: carrots and onions and potatoes, peeled and diced, and into the water they went.

Behind the Pillars

When she had come for the first time to the great front doors of the hospital in New Haven, up the stone steps and through the opening between the pillars, she felt a flicker of recognition. Not that it reminded Margaret of the Dublin Hospital on Baggot Street. There was more of a resemblance to Winston Court, huge and grey and overblown, some grandiose vision that exceeded any possible use for the place.

And once the doors opened that impression did not change. Dark portraits on the walls, and cobwebs in the high corners of the rooms, and the hint of dustiness on most of the surfaces. And the woman coming toward her, down the dim corridor, had looked at her with suspicion, as if seeing an unwelcome intruder in her private domain.

"What are you doing here?"

It was not an auspicious start. That she had come here at all had been something she had thought about for months, waiting and watching as the comedy of indecision in Robert's and Timothy's lives was played out. At first they had simply waited for some great inspiration, sleeping late and then sitting and talking on the porch with John Sullivan, as if someone would walk up to the steps with a summons about some sudden good fortune. And then they both began, reluctantly, to work at the wharf, laborers in the loading and off-loading of ships, something that paid little money and clearly would not lead to anything better. And then suddenly, miraculously, her hapless stepson Timothy, who at times seemed barely sure of his own name, not only found steady employment with a blacksmith's shop but, even more surprising, began courting the young

Catherine Brennan, who thought him not at all a dunce, but rather the most brilliant, and the handsomest, person on the face of the earth. And Robert, so used to having to speak for the two of them and lead the way in even the simplest matters of daily life, seized the moment and escaped, not simply to the other side of New Haven Harbor but on to a ship bound for far-off places, for the Gold Rush in California, wending its way down the coast to Baltimore and Charleston and New Orleans. And he had the misfortune to arrive in New Orleans as yellow fever was raging, and that was the last that they heard of him.

"I came to see Miss Bentley. Is she here?" Margaret had only the woman's name, no image of what she might look like, or what her reception might be. The priest had given her the name, or what he thought to be the name, but he seemed a bit dubious that she would find much of a welcome if she went to the hospital looking for work. The hospital was not a place for their kind.

"And what might you want to see me about?"

The shadowy figure came closer, now looking hard at her from behind wire-rimmed eyeglasses, as if inspecting some kind of alien specimen.

"Miss Bentley, I am Margaret Fogarty, and I have been a hospital nurse, and trained in midwifery as well. I have been in New Haven for some time, and wish to inquire about whether there might be work for me here."

The eyes behind the glasses continued to look hard at her, as if trying to focus in the dimness. "And are you able to read?" The woman seemed somewhat disbelieving that someone with an Irish lilt in her voice could be what she presented herself to be.

"I learned to read and write as a child. I have worked with two different doctors in Ireland, and then as ward nurse and head nurse at the City of Dublin Hospital." She paused. "And trained in midwifery at the Rotunda in Dublin as well."

"Yes. So. We have few patients, and those who come often bring their own nurse." Miss Bentley was not often faced with this kind of query: usually someone at the door was seeking to store possessions, or to put away out of sight an old and troublesome family member who was near death and disruptive to the household. No one in New Haven was quite sure, yet, what a hospital was supposed to be. Stories had been heard of such places in great cities, London or New York or Philadelphia or Boston, but establishing a hospital seemed to require more than just erecting a building.

Edwina Bentley was not herself from New Haven; she had grown up near Boston, and even as a young woman had sought to dedicate herself to good works. Her dream had been to marry a clergyman and to go off with him to serve as missionaries in some distant and exotic and pagan place. But no suitable candidate presented himself, and, if the truth were to be told, she was not very much inclined to marriage. Then someone spoke to her of the need at the new hospital in New Haven for a respectable unmarried woman for a matron, and New Haven seemed just as good as a foreign land, without the same complications of travel.

So she had made the journey, just as the hospital was first opening its doors in 1832, and had moved into the suite of rooms set aside for the matron. And from then to now – almost twenty years – she had rarely ventured forth from the hospital and grounds, except on the Sabbath, when she walked to the church on the Green and back again. What she observed on that walk, less than a mile in each direction, was almost all that she knew of the city around her. The physicians who came to the building, to see patients relegated to its chambers, had little to say to her except directives about the needs of invalids under her care. And the invalids themselves were almost all old cast-off members of the families that had run New Haven since its founding a century and a half earlier. So Edwina Bentley surmised, as they did as well, that little was changing in the world.

That things stayed so much the same was part of the problem. The hospital had been built with the expectation that it would house several dozen patients, some in private rooms, most in wards. But it was rare that there were more than ten or fifteen staying within its walls. When someone came, they stayed – at first receiving visitors and the frequent attentions of a doctor; and then as time went on, having no one look in on them except a family servant or two who brought them supplies and changed their linens and bathed them. Edwina Bentley visited every patient every day, to be sure that they were receiving the care they needed, and that they were still breathing. In extreme cases, she would hire a woman to see to nursing them, and have the bill sent to the family.

Margaret Fogarty appeared before her at a fortuitous moment. The skills and experience that she claimed barely registered as Miss Bentley listened to the newcomer. It was evident that she was an immigrant, but she had been in New Haven long enough that her spoken language was fairly comprehensible; and, in any case, the patient needing assistance was unlikely to voice any objections. Hosea Williams had gone to sea when he was only a boy, and had spent his life there, finally becoming captain of his own ship, only returning to land when he could no longer see or hear, to find that his family loved him no more than when he had run away to sea in the first place. And he had difficulty walking, and frequent fevers, and a host of other maladies that made it seem that life's end was near; yet he kept on living. If someone spoke to him, he answered, but in an irritated and contentious fashion. If asked a question, his answer might have nothing to do with the subject that had been raised.

"Are you aware of the needs of the elderly?" Miss Bentley tried to think of how she could determine that this woman standing before her was suitable, so she could say that she had made a proper search for a nurse before she asked the family for payment for her services. "Can you determine that someone is eating properly? And," she chose another tack, "Do you avoid strong drink yourself? It will be necessary for you to live here at the hospital: are you free to do so, or must you care for others as well?"

Margaret waited for the stream of questions to end. It would not be the same, working here, as it had been at the hospital on Baggot Street; but perhaps things would change, and it would lead to the kind of work she had done before. "I have cared for old people as well as for children," she said. "It was somewhat different in Dublin, where many more people needed hospital care. And yes, I am free to live here. I have no need of strong drink: a cup of tea is what I prefer. I would welcome the chance to use my nursing skills again." She looked directly at Miss Bentley, who still seemed dubious, but could not find any faults that made her a poor choice for looking after Hosea Williams.

"So. I must consult with the patient's family: Captain Hosea Williams is his name, and he has been with us for two months now, and he needs more attention than he currently receives. Come again on the day after tomorrow, and I will know better if we have need of you." She nodded curtly, and turned, and walked off into the shadows. Margaret was left to let herself out, and close the doors behind her.

And so it happened that by the following week she was once again settled in a room of her own in a huge hospital building, her wooden crate in the corner, her shawl folded and laid on top of it. She was not the only one here – the only nurse, that is – but it was so different from Baggot Street. Not every patient had a nurse to himself: some had the attention of a variety of servants from the family household, who came and went caring for their needs. The patients were old people, by and large – not injured, not even sick necessarily. Their common need was that they were beyond caring for themselves.

Margaret's room was her own; but much of her attention was devoted to Captain Williams, in his own room, considerably larger and airier than hers. When she first entered, he was sitting in the chair near the window, a chair with a tall carved back. He did not seem to know that she was there; he was looking out the window, his eyes half open. She made up the bed, and took the water-pitcher to fill it, and straightened the objects lying on the bedside table: brush, comb, pocket-watch, lamp. When she came again two hours later, everything was the same; only the angle of shadows from the window had changed.

"Do you need anything, sir?" she asked. She could not tell if he responded: his head moved slightly, slowly, back and forth, but perhaps he was just shifting in his chair.

Then when she entered the room once again, later in the day, he stirred himself and turned and looked at her.

"Have you ever been to sea?" His voice was low, rough, and it sounded as if it was some time since he had made use of it, and as if he had to search his mind to remember how to form the words, what the words were that he wanted to be speaking.

"Sir, I came to America some time ago. By ship. From Dublin. It was a long hard voyage." She had not spoken of the journey for all this time; it was all behind her, she kept telling herself.

His low voice rumbled; she leaned toward him to catch his words. "On the sea you are free, carried by the wind." He turned his head toward her, clouded eyes glaring, and picked up the cane beside his chair and shook it at her. "Here, I am in a prison!" He turned back toward the window once again.

She said nothing, but went on with her routine tasks: changing the linens on the bed, hanging fresh towels on the hooks beside the door. His head had now fallen to the side against the chair back, and he slept, snoring sonorously. She left the room quietly and closed the door.

The sea: that had been her prison, was what she thought – the place where hope had died, where a part of her spirit had departed from her. She remembered the grey turbulence of the waves, boiling up around the ship, and the creaking of the timbers night and day; and the wind in the flapping sails, the crew hoisting them and lowering them again as the breezes changed direction. It was not fear that she had been feeling on shipboard: it was a sense of abandonment. And now this man, trapped in his chair, in his room, was longing for the world that had been so alien to her.

When she entered the room again, he was awake, but his face was without expression or recognition.

"Where did you sail to, sir? To England? Or to the Continent?"

At first it seemed he had not even heard her. Then the low rumble of his voice came once again. "From Boston to California and the northwest coast. And then, when we had all the skins we could buy, on to Hahwayee and the islands, and then China, and then back again with porcelain and lacquerware and tea. Back and forth a dozen times – not always the same ship: ships fall to rot, and run aground, and then you have to find another one." He fell silent for several minutes. Then he spoke again. "And keep your charts, and your log book: never lose hold of them, or you may never make it home." Once again he paused. "Whatever home is good for: perhaps better not to return at all."

Once again he seemed to have slipped away, into himself, out of reach of conversation. Margaret knew that the evening meal would soon be ready in the kitchen, and that the tray might catch his attention; but it was just as likely that it would sit untouched beside him, left to get cold, until she carried it away once again at twilight. She walked down the hallway from Captain Williams' chamber, past the long room meant to be a ward for a dozen beds but now occupied only by chairs and tables and cabinets stored away by some wealthy family with more accumulations than their house could hold. She thought of the children's ward at Baggot Street, each bed occupied by someone struggling to return to health. She shook her head: such a waste – every time she walked along Morocco Street she saw someone who needed care, hobbling with a walking-stick or an improvised set of crutches. And then there were those who came off a ship already ill, with fever or flux or broken bones poorly-set. But this hospital did not seem to be intended for such as these – the Irish, the Germans, all those who lived outside the domain of propriety of those who had built the place.

The encounters with Miss Bentley had lost something of their unpleasant edge. The Williams family were relieved that their problem had been dealt with, that Captain Hosea was not suffering from neglect. He had no shortage of family members, and they all were living in comfort due in large part to the wealth accumulated from the Captain's voyages to Asia. The otter and beaver pelts brought ample return when they were sold in China. The price of animal skins had appreciated to such a degree that first Hosea Williams' brother Abraham, and then the nephew Nathaniel, became the principals of a bank they established which had brought in its own abundant income. So the house had fine furnishings, and more than a single carriage.

Nathaniel was the most frequent visitor. Perhaps once a week he would appear at the hospital and ask for Miss Bentley, and expect a report on his uncle's welfare. He knew of Margaret's existence – after all, he provided the funds for her salary to be paid – but it had not occurred to him that she might have anything to say about the Captain's health or state of mind. Before he left the hospital each time, he would enter the patient's room and, if Captain Williams was awake, shake his hand and assure him that Abraham had asked after him and sent his best wishes. If Margaret was present, he might nod curtly but not speak to her – what was there to be said? – and then go downstairs again to bid farewell to Miss Bentley.

On one of his visits, he raised a nagging concern, as he was speaking with her. "What of the plans for an invalids' ward here at the hospital? There is no shortage of sick poor to be seen on the streets of New Haven. It is a distraction, even a scandal."

Edwina Bentley drew herself up stiffly. She hardly expected criticism from the Williams family, after the effort she had made to solve their problems. "The space is occupied, and no further plans have been brought to me for ward care. Nursing the indigent would be costly, and funds would have to be provided." She thought mention of money would be enough to quell any concern in this regard.

Nathaniel Williams looked at her steadily: sometimes he wondered if she was the best person to be in charge here. "I will take the matter up with the doctors, when I happen to meet them." He was not really certain about what could be done; but everyone, he knew, was feeling more and more distressed about seeing people on the street who were ill or injured and not even settled, hidden, within their own homes. In the big cities, perhaps, this could be expected, but New Haven should not be in this predicament.

Miss Bentley sincerely hoped that she would hear nothing more about wards and care of the sick poor. However, after the next meeting of the hospital's trustees, two of the doctors made an appointment to see her.

"Some very good news, Miss Bentley. A gentleman has drawn together a number of people willing to support operating a ward for indigent patients here in the hospital. An excellent thing, not just for the college and the medical students, of course, but for the patients, too."

Miss Bentley sat, blinking, her lips pursed. "And what of the goods that are stored there?"

"Some other place will be found. We have three months before the plan will be put in operation. So arrange for the furniture to be moved, and the ward cleaned and painted. And, oh yes, for nursing and house-keeping staff as well." She looked at them, aghast. They rose, and smiled, and donned their hats and left the room.

* * *

A fine situation this is. Everything has been in very good order: quiet, and well managed, and the patients cared for. Trouble-makers they are, always finding fault with the present circumstances. What will be accomplished if we fill the wards with people so sick that they are bound to die a few days after they arrive? In no time our reputation will be ruined. Fine gentlemen, these doctors from the college may be; but their occasional visits do little indeed to care for the people lying here in the beds.

And who will we find to care for all of them? It's one thing to find a nurse for an invalid, but quite another when you have a room full of strangers, none of them acquainted with the person in the next bed, each of them in fear and at death's door. Now Mrs. Fogarty claims to have such experience, but I doubt that she has any more idea than I do how to bring order out of such a mess. Constant comings and goings: the sick coming in, and moaning, and dying, and being carried away. And what will be accomplished by all of it?

* * *

"Nurse Fogarty, I must speak with you." It was rare that Miss Bentley spoke her name; usually there were just curt instructions, issued with as much brevity as she could muster. But this was something different. Miss Bentley beckoned, and led her toward the parlor, the same room where she had heard out the gentlemen the day before.

"How is Mr. Williams' health?"

Had there been some complaint, Margaret wondered? She was becoming attached to him – not that he ever seemed sure why she was there, but he recognized her, and each day would dredge up another anecdote from his past, a bit more of his story. "He seems in good spirits,

Miss, and is eating well. Some days he is not much aware of his surroundings; but he is not unhappy, I believe." She was not sure this answered Miss Bentley's question.

The old man was frail, and each day there seemed to be a bit less of him, as if he was diminishing before her eyes. She took his arm, now, when he moved from chair to bed; the cane was not enough to steady him. Hosea Williams was the only person she had touched in such a long time. Each day she felt less life in him, as if the blood was cooling in his veins. His face was no longer ruddy, as it had been from years of facing the winds. It was becoming almost translucent. And so too with his hands: a spider-web of veins every day more prominent, but less and less color to them.

She came back to the conversation with Miss Bentley. "He is an old man, that is all."

Miss Bentley knew as much. She was less concerned about the person than about keeping the Williams family happy: that would continue to be important long after the old man was gone.

"I must speak to you about another matter. Mr. Williams, of course, is your main duty. But the big room – where the goods are now stored – will soon become a charity ward." She pursed her lips; she could barely bring herself to say the words. "You know something of such things."

Margaret stood quiet for a moment, her hands clasped before her. "It will be a fine ward, Miss. First we remove everything, and then it must be cleaned and painted. And then beds – room for twelve beds, at least, I would think. And linens. And nurses – perhaps two to start with, and a night nurse as well." She was calling up all the details from her memories of Baggot Street. "The laundry – a laundress will be needed. A ward requires clean linens daily. And much more."

Miss Bentley nodded weakly. These were things she had not even thought about. At least she would not seem entirely ignorant when Nathaniel Williams and the doctors came again.

A Plot of Land

"Father Maguire." She spoke his name as soon as he opened the door. "I am Margaret Fogarty, the nurse at the Hospital. I think you know my stepson Timothy and his wife Catherine."

"Ah yes, Mrs. Fogarty, of course. I baptized their latest just last month. Quite a brood they have now." He was about to comment on Margaret's absence from the christening, and the rarity of her appearances at Sunday Mass, but he thought better of it. It was because of her, he knew, that many of his flock were cared for in their final illnesses, that babies were delivered into the world, that people were inoculated when the threat of smallpox revealed itself.

She smiled with pleasure. When she visited the younger Fogartys, on her days off from work, she and Catherine would have a cup of tea, perhaps even a piece of cake, while the small ones climbed on and off their laps, enjoying the extra attention. Timothy often tried to persuade her to come live with them – there was no need for her to go on working, he insisted – but she demurred. She would never be without a child on her lap if she accepted their offer, of that she was certain.

"Father, I came about the cemetery. I wish to purchase a burial plot."

A strange request, he thought, from a widow. Generally it was family men who decided to make provisions for themselves and their kin, purchasing a plot large enough for the remains of a half dozen or so, probably all with the same surname, and a headstone big enough that names and dates could be added over the years.

"Usually the plots are large enough for several burials, you know, Mrs. Fogarty." He did not want to be taking money from a widow – even though he would be happy to see another parcel at St. Bernard's spoken and paid for.

She suppressed a smile. "People are dying all the time, Father. I doubt that I will lie in the plot alone. And this is my home now: best to be sure there a place for me to be laid to rest when my time comes."

He looked at her curiously. He expected a widow to be more submissive, not to talk back to a man of the cloth like himself. Usually when someone came to him to make arrangements – a funeral, a christening, a wedding – it was a man, almost always Irish, often a familiar face, someone whose story he already knew. A few friendly words, a pat on the shoulder, an admonition or two, and exchange of coin before parting. The women were in church, of course, but not too much had to be spoken to them: a nod, perhaps a smile; sometimes raising his hand in a gesture of blessing.

"Will your son be paying for this, then?" He knew that Timothy had all he could do to keep food on the table.

"Not at all, Father. I have the money with me." She put her hand into the small bag she was carrying and pulled out a small stack of dollar bills, and four gold coins removed from her box just that morning. She reached out to hand them to him.

He tried not to look astonished. "This is more than is customary, Mrs. Fogarty. You should not squander what you have: the day may come when you will need it."

"What I need, Father, is to know that I'll not some day be buried in the potter's field."

An unusual woman, this is, he thought. "I will see to it, and have your name assigned to a plot – a good location, in the center and toward the back, with a tree planted in its corner. And the deed will be brought to you as soon as it is prepared."

She rose and drew her shawl around her shoulders. "Thank you, Father. And pray for us all." She turned to leave. He opened the door, and nodded as she departed.

The late afternoon sunlight filtered through the brilliant colors of the remaining leaves, gold and rust and bronze, along the road edge, as she made her way back toward the Hospital. Since the time when the charity ward had first opened – a great upheaval in what had been a quiet, placid place – Margaret Fogarty had become the indispensable resource. Still, without doubt, she was an immigrant, and Irish, and a woman, and a widow: all of those burdensome qualities that made people dismiss her as inconsequential. Even she herself thought that way at times. But, on the other hand, so many things could not happen without her.

Miss Bentley had struggled to reach some resolution in how she thought about the woman. Not that she found her to be insubordinate. Rarely did she have to give her orders or instructions, because Nurse Fogarty usually knew what was to be done before she herself had even formulated what was necessary. And this, indeed, made Miss Bentley more uncomfortable, knowing as she did that she was the one in charge, the person responsible for everything running smoothly. The trustees expected that of her.

In some ways she and the Irishwoman were very much alike – almost the same age; not much different in height. Her hair was graying faster than Margaret's. Both of them wore it pulled back from the face, pinned into a bun; but Miss Bentley's appearance had a severity about it, and Margaret Fogarty's more of a touch of softness – of empathy, perhaps, with those she cared for.

The distance between the two of them never changed. Miss Bentley would have to be the one to make the change, to reach out, and that was not likely to happen. Best things stay the way they were; loneliness was a natural part of things.

Edwina Bentley kept each person she had contact with precisely labeled in her mind, organized in neat categories. Captain Hosea Williams, for instance. He was quite high on her list, not because of any communication that had occurred between herself and him. She could not even be sure that they had ever spoken to each other. But his presence in the hospital had been something of a milestone, evidence that the Hospital could be trusted with the care of a person of prominence. It did not have to be said that no one else wanted him under their roof. But he was well cared for, and everything was in good order, even in his final days. Miss Bentley saw him daily, checked his pulse, notified his family of his steady decline. When the morning came when he did not awaken, she was prepared, and arrangements were made, and the funeral and the burial all properly dealt with.

She was taken aback that morning to see tears in Mrs. Fogarty's eyes. Emotions are not appropriate, she thought to herself. Something only the Irish would sink to, being drawn into maudlin sentiment when there was work to be done. But she said nothing to the woman: there were few things to complain about in how she carried out her duties.

As Margaret re-entered the Hospital after her visit with Father Maguire, Miss Bentley was at the door of the parlor, the place where she met with important people – trustees, physicians, family members of someone recently deceased. Each of them in a neat category.

"Miss Bentley." Margaret raised her voice to catch her attention. "The young boy with the fever: he is much better today, almost ready to leave us, I believe."

The problem with the ward was that there were so many comings and goings. The patients did not just suffer, and decline, and die. One day they were worse, and then better, and expecting to get out of bed and walk the hallways. It was almost impossible to maintain order in such circumstances. Mrs. Fogarty kept track of them all, she knew, but it was not the way Edwina Bentley liked things managed. This boy, for instance – at death's door, delirious, thrashing about, and then in a stupor; and then when the fever broke sleeping for a full two days. And then wide awake, ready to get out of bed and run up and down the halls as if nothing had ever been wrong with him. Miss Bentley had no patience for such goings on: an invalid should act like one, and be grateful for the care provided.

On Sundays, when she went to the big church on the New Haven Green, she sat by herself, always in more or less the same pew. She knew that almost anyone would have welcomed her to join them in their customary place, but she preferred to keep her distance. Otherwise it was too uncomfortable when an acquaintance became a patient. For her, the commitment to virtue dictated that she should keep her own counsel, avoid involvements. The people around her had become accustomed to her remoteness: she was deep in prayer, they assumed, communing with her God. Whether that was the same as their God, they were not sure.

It was perhaps a week after Margaret's meeting with Father Maguire that the visitor came to see her at the Hospital. Miss Bentley inquired what business he had with Mrs. Fogarty and the man replied simply that he was a family member. His dress was not that of a gentleman, but still he had a certain look of prosperity, his hair grey and thinning, his face angular, his hands worn from work.

"She is at work, with the patients in the ward, and has much to do," Miss Bentley stated, none too gently. "You could leave your name, perhaps."

"I'd rather wait," he said. "I have come a long way, and it's today that I'd like to see her." He sat down, his cap placed on the small table beside him.

She thought about what else she might say, how to avert some planned invasion, and then decided it was best to say nothing. She turned stiffly and left the parlor.

The afternoon passed, and the light faded early, as happens in the final weeks of the years. Margaret was weary as the twilight came, ready for a quiet cup of tea, and not expecting the announcement from the matron that someone was waiting to see her in the parlor. Another inquiry about a patient, she anticipated, and whether recovery was a likelihood or even a possibility. The room was dim as she entered, only one lamp lit and the glow from the fireplace casting shadows.

The man stood up as she stopped in the doorway, and took a step toward her. "Maggie, do you remember me?" he said. "I'm Frank. Francis Fogarty."

She stood frozen. She looked hard at him, trying to see the young man who had captivated her for those few hours, whose image had been cherished through all the years between.

"Frank." She spoke slowly. "I didn't know if you were even alive. When we came here. . . ." her voice trailed off.

He came and took her hand gently, just for a moment or two. "I have always had you on my mind," he said and then let her hand go again.

She gestured back toward the chairs, and then seated herself, waiting for him to do the same. "So, Francis. Tell me about where you live, and all that you have been doing. Have you seen Timothy? Would you have known him as your own brother?" She spoke lightly, so as not to show the turmoil inside her.

"He told me where to find you. You look just the same, Maggie; nothing has changed."

Nonsense, she thought; I'm an old woman now. But he is as fine to look at as he was that night.

"Near Saratoga is where I live: horse country, with fine rolling fields, and hills in the distance. Almost twenty years ago I went there, first as a blacksmith, and then a handler. And then as luck would have it, I came into some land; and now a few horses of my own, breeding and raising and training them." He stopped and smiled. "Trying to outdo my father, perhaps. I learned it mainly from Patrick Fogarty, truth to be told."

"And where is Saratoga?"

"Two hundred miles or more, off to the northwest, north of Albany in New York State. Cold and harsh in the winters, but beautiful too; and a great place for the horse races." He paused for a minute or two. "It's a long journey, but I had to come and see if you were here."

"Here indeed I am, Francis, and with no shortage of things to keep me busy. It's becoming a real hospital now, with the sick being brought here and getting proper care. The kind of thing I know how to do – what I learned in Roscrea, and in Dublin."

They sat quietly for a few minutes, the crackle of the flames in the fireplace the only sound.

"Why don't you come away, Maggie, up to the mountains. I'll build you a house, a cottage of your own, with space for a garden, and a coop for chickens if you want. No need for you to go on working, living alone in a room up under the roof. Put all that behind you, Maggie." His eyes on her, gentle, pleading. "Think about it, Maggie. I'll be back tomorrow to see you." He stood up, his cap in his hand, reluctant to turn and leave.

Margaret had her hands still clasped in her lap, one thought after another tumbling through her mind. Then she stood, and reached out a hand and laid it on his arm. "It's so good to see you, Francis. And tomorrow I'll have some tea for you, and we can talk."

She walked with him to the door, and watched as he went down the front steps and off into the dark.

She turned away again after she had closed the great door, putting a hand against the wall to steady herself for a moment, and then climbed up the stairs, past the ward, and up another flight to her own room. Not that there was any elegance to it, any permanence; but she lived here, with the few familiar objects. A teapot; a wooden crate, holding her treasures; a shelf of books, carried with her through the years from place to place. The room had a snugness to it, a worn comfortable feel to the bed and chair and table. When she needed a change of scene, a few hours with Catherine and Timothy was enough to drive her back once again.

In the morning of the next day the weak winter sun glimmered on the windowsill. During the night she had dreamed of chickens, pecking at the pathway as she walked toward a cottage, not a familiar cottage but a place she had never seen before. The chickens were not a welcoming flock: they seemed more menacing, as if defending their territory from an interloper. She rose and dressed, pulling her mind back to the affairs closer at hand. Last night's visitor she pushed from her thoughts, concentrating instead on bandages, on crutches, on the woman with the broken leg, someone who needed to learn to walk again. Something so familiar, then forgotten, needing to be learned anew.

She stood beside the bed, holding the crutches as the woman awkwardly turned, letting the leg with the cast on it drop toward the floor. It was heavy, and it threw her off balance as she tried to stand. Margaret held the crutches firmly, parallel, until the woman regained her equilibrium and reached for them, grimacing, determined. Then she resolutely pulled herself to her feet and stood, a crutch supporting her under each arm, and gave Margaret a weak victorious smile.

The boy with the fever had gone home healthy, and new patients appeared, today like every day. Each person a different story, a crisis, a problem to be solved, wounds to bandage and medicines to administer, charts to record every detail, physicians to hear out, surgeons to give further instructions.

The woman with the crutches was half her age, someone with a fragmented life, her broken leg only a small part of what was broken. Her story was also torn to pieces, and Margaret had only captured bits of it, as she heard what might happen next once she could walk again. No secure, snug room or her own; no place where it was certain that she could lay her head and pull a coverlet over her. Perhaps her best good fortune was that she had broken her leg, and some fate had brought her to the ward where the leg could mend and she could sleep in a warm dry bed.

One patient after another, and bandages, and medicines, and changing bed-linens, and folding towels. She was immersed in all of it, and the hours passed, the shadows and sunlight moving from one window to another to another.

Miss Bentley appeared suddenly before her, distracting her from the work at hand.

"Nurse Fogarty, that man is here again, asking after you. This is not proper: he must not be bothering you." She did not want to press her: what would happen if suddenly she was no longer here? "Do you want me to tell him to go away?" The two women stood, more aware of each other and the distance between them than they ever had been.

Margaret finished folding the pile of cloth before her, gathering herself together.

"It is not a problem, Miss Bentley. He has come a long way, and it is important that I talk with him again. I promised him tea." She knew that Miss Bentley was unhappy with all of this, rigid with fear about unfamiliar interlopers.

"Be sure the door is bolted when he leaves." She pursed her lips, and turned on her heel, and left the hallway.

Margaret gathered herself before she went down to the parlor; she saw to it that a kettle was hot, and cups and a teapot ready, and carried them with her as she entered the room.

"Francis: it is good of you to come again." She set it all down on the table, carefully hiding any nervousness, keeping her eyes upon the tray.

"Maggie, will you come away with me?" He could not put his time into pleasantries – it was all that he had thought about for months and years.

She jostled the pot a bit before pouring the tea into the cups.

"I think of you every day, Francis, and of the time when we met." She raised her eyes, and looked steadily at him. "It might have been different, when I first arrived here, or even a few years ago. But now – I cannot leave: this is where my life is, my work, the place where I am needed." She stopped talking, and handed him the cup of tea, and a spoon for the sugar. "It would be so lovely to see you every morning. As you are always in my mind's eye."

"You'll change your mind, Maggie: I'll come again, and you'll think better of the offer." He smiled, almost desperately, and took her hand between his.

"You'll be welcome whenever you come, Francis."

The Wounds of Battles

Suddenly everything was in turmoil. The hospital was not as it had been – sedate, quiet, orderly. It was not that what needed to be done had changed. Always, there would be the old, the injured, the fevered; but now the War had thrown all of that into the background.

Everyone knew about the War, though the battles were something in the distance, off in places in Pennsylvania and Maryland and Virginia. Conscription called upon those close at hand. Timothy was too old; his sons were too young. But so many others – some with excitement, some in fear and trembling – were drafted, and mustered, and marched off to the south and west.

"Margaret. I must speak with you." She had never used her given name to speak to her before: Margaret was not even sure that she knew it. And so she turned, and they met eye to eye, and she followed Miss Bentley into the parlor.

"The patients are all to be moved." Miss Bentley had her hands clasped, wringing them together before her. "The hospital – it is to house sick and wounded soldiers, hundreds of them, I do not know how." She had a frantic look about her. "Tents, they say, and volunteers to nurse the patients: and I am to organize it all." Her voice raised in pitch, but faded in volume, as if diminishing into some edge of madness.

"Margaret – Mrs. Fogarty – a house is to be found for our present patients, but they must be transported, and their care provided for. And you, I would hope, will take care of it all." Miss Bentley smiled, nervously, a hint of unbalance once again glittering in her eyes. The War was so far away from Connecticut: why should the serenity of her days be disrupted?

"What kind of house? And where? And when?" Margaret tried to absorb the very complicated idea, moving the handful of ailing individuals now within their walls, and all the things needed to care for them, and then starting over in a different place. And even more unimaginable, pitching tents on the grounds around the hospital building, and carrying in dozens of prostrate forms on stretchers – hundreds, Miss Bentley had said – and then producing out of thin air everything needed for their care, their return to health, or at least their decent burial.

"The house: do you know where it will be?" Margaret went over the list of current patients in her mind – how many beds, how many rooms; who could be transported easily, and who would present difficulties. For some it would be a welcome adventure, but not for everyone.

"Mr. Nathaniel Williams says he has a building in mind, and that we will know in two or three days, certainly by the end of the week." Miss Bentley twisted a handkerchief nervously in her hands. "Perhaps we can just discharge the patients – some of them, at least." She did not love challenges, even simple ones, and this upheaval had an enormity to it.

"And we must have staff: a cook, a laundress, nurses. The ones we have here: can they be moved as well, or must they remain?" Margaret was thinking out loud, as much as she was hoping for answers.

"Everything will be provided, the Committee says: funds will be raised, supplies provided, payments made. I just don't know," Miss Bentley said, plaintively, helplessly.

"First things first," Margaret said briskly, as she stood up. "I will start a list, and draw up a plan. Once we know about the building, we will have a better idea what is to be done."

The parlor was dim, with lamp flames casting wavering shadows, and outdoors the murk of late afternoon at the edge of winter was as dark. A cold dampness hung in the air, and fingers of fog crept inland from the harbor. It was tempting to stay indoors, and avoid the clammy grip of twilight. But Margaret went up to her room, and put on her cloak and shawl and gloves, and set off to visit Catherine and Timothy for a brief escape, for a cup of tea and the noise of children. It was still dry underfoot – no mud to slip on, blessedly – and the street lamps would be alight by the time she returned. The streets were quiet, with only an occasional horse or cart or carriage, and few people on foot beside herself. Everything was familiar, as if she had lived here and passed this way forever: she could walk the few blocks with her eyes closed, had it been necessary to do so. The great pillared building and the small house on Morocco Street – her lifeline was suspended between the two, and she held firmly to the line.

She climbed the front steps, pulling her shawl down from around her head as she opened the door. "Catherine: have you water hot for a cup of tea?" she called as she entered. In an instant, children were upon her, hugging, pulling at her skirt, demanding to be picked up and carried with her. One, two three, four, five, six – each visit it seemed there were more of them.

Catherine and Margaret were sitting at the kitchen table with their tea, each with a child in their laps, when Timothy returned, the grime of the forge on his hands and face and clothes.

"They're moving Margaret's hospital, would you believe." Catherine spoke first, before he even had his hat removed from his head.

"Well, you'll come live with us, then. Such foolishness, to move a hospital. And you're not young, besides: time to take your ease, Ma, and enjoy being a grandmother."

She knew what he was saying, that he meant it for the best: but the adventure before her was irresistible. "Some day, some day, Timothy, but not now. They <u>need</u> me, you know: how would it all happen if I were not there?"

Their eyes locked for a moment: she thinks too much of herself, he thought.

She walked back to the hospital again within the hour, thinking about where to start. Nothing could begin before she went to see the house, and then it would need to be cleaned and furnished: a few days at the very least before supplies and patients could be moved.

It was Friday morning when she was called once again to the parlor. Nathaniel Williams was sitting with Miss Bentley, and he was speaking as she entered: ". . . Vacant since the owners died, but still completely furnished. Everything covered with dust, of course, but that is easily remedied. And the goods that are not needed can be stored in the barn. I have spoken with the doctors at the college, and they find it quite acceptable – as convenient a location for them as this one is."

Miss Bentley turned slightly to acknowledge Margaret's presence. "Would you be so kind as to take Mrs. Fogarty to see the house? She will be in charge of getting it ready, and once she has been through it we will know better how quickly the patients can be moved."

Nathaniel nodded and rose to his feet. "Of course, of course." He picked up his hat and walking stick. "Come along: let us do it right now. I have the morning free."

Margaret left to get her cloak and gloves.

Miss Bentley spoke again to Nathaniel, barely above a whisper. "She is an immigrant, you know, and Irish, but really quite trustworthy and intelligent in spite of it. The best we can do, at the moment."

He said nothing, but waited for Margaret's return, and then led the way toward the door.

They walked side by side for the short distance, about a half mile, to the large dark house – almost a mansion, but much smaller than the hospital. He pulled an ornate key from his pocket, and unlocked the great front door. It creaked on its hinges as it swung open. Light trickled in through the window at the back of the hallway, but aside from that everything was dark: dark carpets, huge somber cabinets; brown patterned wallpaper, paneling and moldings and door- and window-frames of stained walnut. The veneer of dust brought the only touch of paleness, catching the sunlight from the window.

They walked from room to room without speaking. Damask and velvet drapes; one piece of large heavy furniture after another. When they returned to the hallway, she turned and faced him.

"Well. There is much to be done. Can the furniture be removed? Everything must be scrubbed, dusted; the windows must be cleaned, the draperies taken down. Fresh air, you know: so important for recovery. The kitchen will do, once it is put in order, and the laundry room also. The servants' rooms above are adequate for three staff."

"The furnishings, yes: they can all go into the barn. The draperies should be put in storage: dampness would ruin them in short order." He liked the way she set out her mental lists: she was quite equal to the task.

"Now, for myself," she said somewhat diffidently. "I do not see any proper place for my accommodations."

He had not really thought about this – that she, also, must live somewhere.

"Let me make inquiries. I know of a house on Rose Street, quite respectable, with rooms for rent. It is close at hand, both to this place and to the hospital. A suite of rooms, a bedroom and a parlor, should be available. If that would meet your needs."

She inclined her head. "I should like to see it, to be sure. But that would be quite fine, Mr. Williams."

They walked back to the hospital. Miss Bentley bustled toward them as they entered.

"Mrs. Fogarty will have it all in order in no time at all." Nathaniel Williams clapped his hands together. "In the morning I will send a crew of workmen to meet her at the house and follow her instructions."

Each morning she rose before dawn, and left the hospital at first light. The house was transformed – bare floors, draperies taken down, every-thing scrubbed; window-panes now gleaming. The walls of the upper rooms, where the patients would be housed, were painted white, and the kitchen shelves were stocked with pots and pans and ladles. Cabinets and closets had folded linens stacked in them, and the small room next to the kitchen, once the butler's pantry, became the storeroom for ban-dages and ointments and medications of every sort. Less than a hospital, she thought, but it will have to do. And each night when she returned through the hospital gate, other changes were evident: platforms erected, and storage sheds, and tents covering most of the grounds, and a wooden barracks being built on one side of the entry walk to serve as a ward.

Miss Bentley was in the midst of it all, standing wringing her hands as the work went on around her. Margaret came and went, virtually unno-ticed: if any one of the new people saw her at all, they looked at her with suspicion – a foreign interloper, not part of the chain of command; some-one answering to no one. And the new women, the nurses, all in similarly drab dress, awaited the orders of surgeons in some sort of uniform, who had some grasp of the monumental challenges that were before them – whether or not they could be met.

When a week had passed the patients were moved – only a dozen of them, two of the oldest having expired amidst the excitement, three others sufficiently improved that they could recover at home. And Margaret played escort, back and forth and back and forth, and then packed her own belongings and moved her own abode, her household contained in a wooden box, to the rooms on Rose Street – a bit dingy, but quiet, with sunshine coming in the streaked windows and a door going into the rooms at the top of the dim stairway, with a good sturdy lock on it, and a kettle atop the small stove that heated the room.

At the house now filled with patients, she was to be in charge, as much as anyone was. The doctors would come and go, as their patients required attention or as Margaret called upon them in a crisis. A routine would quickly emerge, much as it had before. But the hospital itself was another matter. An Army surgeon was to be in charge, assigning resources as each new wave of wounded soldiers arrived, giving orders to the nurses and other staff, trying to channel the efforts of the well-intentioned family members of the sick and wounded, and blaming everything that went awry, from onset of gangrene and dysentery to shortages of bandages, on the poor Miss Bentley. It was rare that amputations had to be performed – most of that had taken place close to the battlefield where the soldiers had fallen. But the infections, and the fevers, and the slow or rapid decline toward death of so many who were brought there, overwhelmed any sense that a hospital was mainly a place to be healed.

And so much of the comings and goings between the great pillars, through the doors, were of grief-stricken relatives coming to collect the remains of a son or a brother who had been loved and had marched off to war and who was now to be buried. For some, the arrangements were simply made for them to be laid in a church graveyard or cemetery not far from New Haven. And for some, it seemed, there was no easy option.

Miss Bentley spoke to Margaret about one of these. "Only a few months he had been here in America, just off the boat from Ireland, so to speak, and he took the place of someone who paid him, so he could send the money home for others to follow. Philip McGann is his name: no one to bury him, and no money to pay even for a plot, much less a stone with his name on it."

Margaret thought for a moment. "I need to speak to Father Maguire first, but perhaps some provision can be made."

Rather than going directly back to her patients, she took a detour and went to the Rectory beside the church and rang the bell.

"Father Maguire, I think you remember me: the nurse, Margaret Fogarty. I paid you for a plot at St. Bernard's. And now there is someone who needs to be buried in it: a young soldier, Philip McGann, dead of his wounds and with no family here."

"And kin of yours, Margaret?"

"No, simply a stranger, but it's good use of the land, and the least I can do." Some mother's son, if not hers; and the solace of being laid in the earth, and not in a watery grave.

He thought it a bit irregular; but so many things were irregular in times like these.

"It will be mid-day tomorrow before the grave will be dug. If you can have the body transported, I will be there at noon to say the prayers. The grave-diggers must be paid, of course."

She nodded, and gathered her cloak around her, and pulled the door closed as she left.

Rose Street

Spring comes slowly in New Haven, with more moisture than sunshine. The War was over, and the Hospital was slowly returning to what it had been before. The tents had been dismantled and folded and carried away. The wooden barracks were yet to be demolished, but at least the edges of the property were no longer cluttered with wagons and makeshift ambulances and grazing horses. Mud still dominated grass, but as the weather warmed there would be more greenery underfoot. Inside, the great hallway was filled with piles of stretchers, and the building had an exhausted feel to it, as if its resources had been stretched beyond all limits.

Miss Bentley was still in residence, but more as a listless observer of the events about her than as a participant. The years of turmoil, of surgeons in uniform giving orders, of other men in uniform lying in hospital beds, of women in drab dresses bustling amidst the ill and the wounded, following the surgeons' orders, had left her with little recognition or respect or authority. And now, as all the military trappings were disappearing and being carried away, it seemed hard to imagine what would happen next.

Hundreds of patients on a single day – as many as six hundred, the Committee records said – all of that was vanishing along with the tents and stretchers and ambulances. But having experienced all that, it seemed unlikely that the Hospital would go back to being mainly the sedate hospice for a dozen or so old men.

Margaret still lived on Rose Street. The days and months there had now stretched into years. In the mornings she walked to the house that was used for the local patients, and in the evenings back home again. And on Sunday afternoons, when the weather was favorable, she took the longer walk to the cemetery, and carefully weeded around the small stone reading "Philip McGann", sometimes in season planting a few seeds to grow flowers, and as she knelt there shedding tears for a young man who she had never known, who sometimes seemed to be everything, everyone, she had held dear and then lost in life.

On those days she did not go to Timothy and Catherine's house for tea, but kept to herself, turning inward, feeling that perhaps the end of things was approaching. She was not young. Her face had changed little, but her hair was greyer, her hands more wrinkled and worn, her step slower by just a bit than it had been when she first came to the Hospital.

When she encountered Miss Bentley, on the days when she visited the great building, the distance between the two of them remained; but now the distance was more the product of forgetfulness than disdain.

"Yes?" Miss Bentley looked up vaguely when Margaret appeared at the parlor door.

"Good morning. I was wondering if a date had been set yet for moving our own patients back here."

A somewhat confused look on Miss Bentley's face made Margaret wonder if she had spoken clearly. Perhaps she is becoming hard of hearing, she thought.

"Nathaniel Williams will be here tomorrow. He is in charge of all decisions."

Margaret could not tell whether this was the answer to her question, or the rote reply which was given to all queries. She nodded to Miss Bentley and went on toward the store room, to see what supplies might still be there to carry back with her. It seemed it might be weeks, even months, before the move could be made.

The following day, Margaret once again walked to the Hospital. Perhaps no one knew any answers about what would happen next. The departure of the hundreds of wounded soldiers was, after all, very recent, and the building itself still had to heal. So too everyone needed to recover strength and energy, all those who had been caught up in nursing the fallen – binding up broken bodies, struggling with outbreaks of smallpox, burying the dead, consoling the bereft. All this had ended, but the new day had not yet dawned.

When she entered the room, Mr. Williams was sitting at the table in the parlor, using it as a desk, with piles of paper in front of him. There were still accounts to be settled with the Army. The enormity of it all still stunned him at times – so many hundreds of soldiers had passed through the doors every month, and the calculations had to be completed of how much money still was owed to the Hospital. And the doctors at the medical school were impatient, needing a place to bring their students to examine patients once again. The last of anyone's concerns seemed to be who was sick now, who in the city needed care. A weariness overwhelmed him. He thought nostalgically of the days when a trip to the Hospital was simply a visit to the cantankerous Hosea Williams.

"Mr. Williams, sir." The woman at the parlor door looked familiar: it was the old Irish woman, the one who had cared for his uncle.

"Yes?"

"Miss Bentley said I was to ask you about the plans."

"Plans?"

"For moving the patients back, sir."

Oh yes: this was the person living in the room on Rose Street. So many details, things that should really be taken care of by someone else.

"We should know in a few days."

"Sir?"

He looked up, a bit impatient.

"Am I to live here once again?"

She did not know what made her ask, or what answer she wanted to hear.

He looked at her blankly. "Of course, you will have to live here: where else?"

She looked at him steadfastly. "I have a family, sir. Grandchildren, who are growing – perhaps it would be best. . ."

He interrupted before she could complete what she was about to say. "Miss Bentley – you know of course that she manages everything, but we have assumed that you could be relied upon, and not just leave us without notice. Reliability is essential, you must know that."

She lowered her eyes and did not speak for a minute or more. When she gathered her courage, her voice was barely audible. "It is not the work, sir; I am happy to work. But I must have a home: the time has come when I must have a home." Before he could say anything she turned and left; if tears came to her eyes they would be tears of anger, and nothing would be served by that.

After she had left, Nathaniel Williams drummed his fingers on the table with some irritation. He should not have to concern himself with these matters. Miss Bentley had been provided with a comfortable life – more than just comfortable, it seemed to him, with her name held in respect by many who did not know how little she actually did, how little her heart seemed to be in the place. The War had been a difficult period for everyone, he knew that, but now was the time to move on, to return to normalcy. Even without the War, the hospital was sorely needed. The city was bustling. It was a quiet place no longer, with new factories and workshops opening almost every month. And workplaces meant injuries, and the people who he knew well – the people who ran the factories – expected their careless workmen to be bandaged up and made whole again at his hospital. That took more than a building, more than the doctors from the medical college. It took these accursed women to nurse people back to health, something far more important than their moods and presumptuous outbursts. Any reasonable man would agree, he thought.

At the end of the day, when Margaret returned to her home on Rose Street, the mood of irritation still weighed upon her. This had been a comfortable place to live, she thought to herself, but it was hardly her own. Each of the several rooms was occupied by someone like herself, a transient, someone waiting for permanence, for calm, for a home.

Rose Street itself had changed little since she came to it: only the people in the houses changed. The houses were not large, not elegant, but they were solid enough. The street itself was not a major thoroughfare. It was just a few hundred feet long, with a sharp change of angle mid-way, and in the early morning most of its residents would set forth from their doorways to various workplaces, factories and shops and forges, the majority of them in the direction of the harbor. Most of the laborers were men, but a few women went on their way to homes and offices, where they would take up their brooms or rolling-pins or feather-dusters. Margaret was the only one on Rose Street who was attached to the Hospital, although it was close at hand. She would be loathe to leave the quiet street to once again live in a room tucked high in the same building where she worked, almost if not quite a prisoner there.

As the months had passed, Miss Bentley's universe was more and more contained within the walls of the building. Of a Sunday morning, she often forgot to don her cloak and bonnet and set off for church. After watching the upheaval around her during the War years, turmoil that seemed to be resolved through the efforts of others, there was less and less reason to do anything at all. And now, with the Hospital at least temporarily empty of patients, and with the Committee holding oversight of the renovation work, the painting and cleaning and moving of furnishings, it seemed she hardly needed to exist. She had become a wraith, barely visible, her complexion and her costume paler from week to week, her voice less audible, her opinions counting for nothing in the things going on around her. Nathaniel Williams pursed his lips with annoyance every time he saw her, but there was really little that a reasonable man could do about it. Once Mrs. Fogarty was back in the building it would be less of a problem: there would be someone then to give orders to, someone to deal with the details.

One Sunday afternoon, Margaret went first to the cemetery – not for long, but just to take the air, and to stop for a moment with a hand on Philip McGann's gravestone and say a prayer, for him, perhaps, and for herself as well. And then she went on, along the streets and lanes that led to Morocco Street, and up the front steps to Timothy and Catherine's. The door was ajar, for the days were getting warmer, but not yet to the point that the air was full of insects. It was a quiet day, except for the dogs barking along the street as she approached. And then, from inside the house, laughter, and a stranger's voice – vaguely remembered, not quite a stranger. An extra person at the kitchen table, a child on the lap of each adult, and other children hanging on the backs of chairs.

"Look who's here, Margaret," said Catherine. "Francis, would you believe! And with a thousand stories, most of them quite incredible."

He stood and turned to greet her, with a broad smile: a bit greyer, but as handsome as ever.

"You're looking wonderful, Maggie." He reached out and took her hand between his. "And still working, is it? Time to start another life, I would think. The offer's still open." He looked at her knowingly, and she could feel the color rising in her face.

"And could I have a cup of tea, Catherine." She took off her shawl, and made her way to the one empty chair on the far side of the table. As soon as she sat down there was a child in her lap as well.

Francis lowered himself into his chair and resumed the story he had been telling – as might be predicted, it had to do with horses and unexpected outcomes. It was less the story than his way with words: even the children, who might not understand at all what he was talking about, kept their eyes glued on him, fascinated by his presence.

And the end of the story came, and then the laughter, and then he turned to Margaret, now stirring her tea. "And what about your life, Maggie? Are they still keeping you busy?"

So she tried to lay it all out, about the War and the wounded and the young man under the small gravestone, about moving patients back and forth from one building to another, about the fading of Miss Bentley and the persistence of the things that she loved about nursing. And about how little she wanted once again to be living in a room in the high reaches of the Hospital, however much she might be dedicated to the rest of it. It did not all make sense, she realized, as the words tumbled out of her, but it was the first chance she had had to speak her mind about all of it. The children stirred restlessly, but even they did not leave. There was a certain magnetic field about what she was saying, about what held them together around the table, that even held their Uncle Frank with his great good looks and his jokes and his stories.

So finally she stopped, and said, "So that's the whole of it. I love the work, but I need so much to have a door I can close as well, and leave all of the work and turmoil outside." Timothy and Catherine and Francis all reached out to her with their eyes, with no words to add, and then Catherine said, "Well. Plenty of stew for all of us, and bread and butter as well, and then some cake." Which broke the spell, and the dishes and cutlery were set all around, and everyone's attention turned to the eating rather than the words.

Once the meal was cleared away and the dishes washed, the parents coaxed the children one by one to their beds, and Margaret, reluctantly, picked up her shawl to leave.

"I'll walk you home, Maggie," said Frank, and took her arm into his as they went out the door and down the steps. He started talking again of Saratoga, of the hills in the distance and the snows almost melted, and the mares with their spindly young colts standing in the fields. Just as Patrick would have done.

"So when do you go back?" she asked.

"Three or four days – some business yet to take care of, but before I leave I'll be seeing more of you for sure." He gave her a quick embrace as they reached her house on Rose Street, and then he turned back the way they had come as she went inside.

As the week started, she threw herself into the work to be done. The move back to the Hospital was getting closer, that was clear – perhaps two weeks, perhaps three, but certainly not more than that. Once again, the wards were taking shape in the big building, with rows of beds and fresh-painted walls and clean polished windows. Some of the private rooms were readied; and the surgical theater, far better equipped than it had been in the days before the War, was waiting to be put to use. And new staff were being hired as well. Three of the women, nurses from the recent War years, were staying, although they seemed quite dubious about both Miss Bentley and Margaret. They would have to see who was giving the orders, and how to interpret them: they made that quite clear.

Less than a dozen patients would need to be transferred from the old house to the Hospital. Each of them had his own story, and Margaret knew how easy it was for the stories to be forgotten. She would not let that happen: no one else beside herself could make sure of it. Different doctors, different nurses – the stories would be lost so easily.

Nathaniel Williams saw her coming and going, seeming always to know what was to be done. One moment he thought her just an incompetent underling; the next he knew that things could barely go on without her. Rarely were words exchanged between them.

At twilight on Tuesday, as she left to return to Rose Street, she found Francis waiting for her. "You work too hard, Maggie."

"Some days I do. But it needs to be done, and I love it, too."

They walked in silence for a few minutes, and then as they neared the house on Rose Street, he pulled something out of his pocket and handed it to her: folded papers.

"What's this?"

"Something for you."

Strange legal documents, something unfamiliar. A deed, with her name on it, it appeared to be; the address was on Rose Street, but not the house she now lived in. She looked at him questioningly.

"The horses have been very good to me, and I hardly know what to do with the money. I heard about this house – it's small, but snug, and enough for you with a room or two to spare. A place just for you, and not far from Timothy and Catherine and the children, when you need companionship."

Indeed, she knew the house: just a few doors from where she was living. She struggled, reaching for words.

"I loved Patrick, you know. Every day I think of him, all these years he has been gone." It was hard even to say his name.

"I loved him too, but he got the best of the bargain." He gave a short laugh, and kicked a rock at the side of the path.

"You'll always have a place to stay when you come to town; you know that." She had not even seen the inside of the place, but already she was unpacking the wooden box, hanging up her clothes, lining up the books on a shelf. She took his arm. "Tomorrow," she said, "I must tell Mr. Nathaniel Williams that I have found a place to live."

ACKNOWLEDGMENTS

Many Long Years to Home is a work of fiction. Its inspiration, Margaret Hickey Fogarty, was my great-great-grandmother, but the story I have pieced together largely comes out of my imagination. The "real person" was indeed born in 1797, and migrated from Ireland to New Haven, Connecticut in 1844 or 1845, just before the great famine in Ireland. She did indeed die in 1870, and is buried in St. Bernard's Cemetery in New Haven.

The story that I have set down is created from the rich trove of materials available in the several medical and hospital libraries in Dublin, as well as the New Haven Colony Historical Society library in New Haven, and the New York Academy of Medicine library in New York City. Bits and pieces of family lore passed down, particularly from my late aunt – another Margaret Fogarty (1909 - 1991) – helped shape the context. And during my visits to Dublin and County Tipperary, Dr. Anne Buttimer and Dr. Jacinta Prunty of University College Dublin, and local historians Kathleen Moloughney and William J. Hayes in Roscrea, helped guide my exploration of public health, hospitals and social life in Ireland and amongst Irish immigrants to North America. Christopher Pryslopski of the Hudson River Valley Institute gave invaluable assistance in locating graphic materials for the book cover. Colin Rolfe of Monkfish Book Publishing Company provided the guidance to turn the manuscript into a "real book.: My thanks to all of these.

And I am especially indebted to my four children, who gave me the plane ticket for that first research expedition to Ireland in 1995; and to my dear husband and partner, Harvey K. Flad, who endured the prolonged struggle to see this work through to publication.

Mary M. Flad
Poughkeepsie NY
August 2024

www.ingramcontent.com/pod-product-compliance
Lightning Source LLC
Chambersburg PA
CBHW031235260626
47169CB00007B/2302